THE TIME THE CHILDREN DIDN'T GO TO SCHOOL

ANNABELLE HAYES

Dearest Emma,

Happy Reading!

Much love,

Annie xxx

FOREWORD

In March 2020, schools, nurseries and colleges in the United Kingdom were shut down in response to the ongoing coronavirus pandemic. By 20 March, all schools in the UK had closed to all children except those of key workers and children considered vulnerable. After a month of numbness at having all the children home, I started these diaries to document the unprecedented time when the children didn't go to school. When the world stopped, the children didn't – this records their time and how they spent it.

I dedicate this book to a very special girl, Lizzie Bramall, who tragically died a week before her 10th birthday in November 2018 of an incurable brain tumour. We miss her every day. She is the girl that didn't get to experience the time they didn't go to school but we wish with every part of our being that she had. Her amazing parents, Sally and Mark, have raised incredible amounts of money with *Lizzie's Fund* for *The Brain Tumour Charity*, organising numerous events and to do something positive in Lizzie's memory for research into a cure. A minimum of ten per cent of the sales from this book will go to this amazing and worthy charity.

ACKNOWLEDGEMENTS

I must thank three very special children, mine, without whom there would have been no content or stories to share. The Teenager, the Middle Child and the Against All Odds Girl (we were convinced we were having another boy) and the other one in my life – the Husband. I love you very much. To my parents, Robert and Elizabeth, thank you for never asking me to 'be or do more' and to my sister, Emma, who provides never ending support and much hilarity too.

Thank you also to Tabitha Peters, Sophie Williams, the Against All Odds Girl and Oli Manson, four young and incredibly talented artists who provided such a great childhood lens of this pandemic with their amazing drawings. You have brought my stories and the history of this time to life with your vivid illustrations and sketches, both of the nature that you observed during the time when we stopped to notice and of the changes to our world as you saw it. A huge thanks goes to Charlie Oliver, who has given over his time to turn my words into works of grammatically correct and well punctuated sentences. I cannot thank you enough for your research, support and hard work.

A final thanks to all my readers, friends and family who have supported my cathartic writing of this time and given me the courage to put my ramblings into a book.

Annabelle x

APRIL 2020

20 April, 2020 – Joe Wicks Workouts and Sharpie Pens

The United Kingdom reported 563 deaths within the past 24 hours, bringing the total number to 2,352. The country's youngest reported person to die of the virus was a 13-year-old boy named Ismail Mohamed Abdulwahab.

Online applications for the Coronavirus Job Retention Scheme are opened, with 67,000 claims registered in the first 30 minutes.

(Wikipedia, 2020)

It's Monday, the WhatsApp groups are going wild, as if no one has been to sleep. I'm collecting memes at the same rate the government is buying up ventilators. It has become the trend for everyone on the groups to reply to each 'funny' in a 'I WhatsApp, therefore I am,' Descartes reassurance. Every time I look again the total of unread messages has quadrupled, I decide to silence all the groups, but half an hour later suffer from a (fear of missing out) FOMO panic and can't resist peeking, only to start the whole 'silencing' process again.

The Against All Odds Girl is refusing to do the Joe Wicks workout – she no longer finds the bunny hops or Spiderman lunges enjoyable and would rather roll about on the sofa asking if it's snack time, despite the fact that only half an hour ago we had a nutritious breakfast of bread and Nutella (we skipped Jamie Oliver's healthy cooking online lessons). The Middle Child agrees but only so he can buy himself Xbox time.

My client is messaging me on a variety of mediums to ask how the article I am writing is going – I am assuming by the frequency of the messages and the fact that he has now stretched to LinkedIn messaging he really would like an answer to this question. I look at the already fed up children and the timetable that I have drawn up and realise that the negotiation time it will take to make them do the timetable and then to actually execute it, drag the 13-year-old out of bed and off his phone, will far outweigh the neatly 30 minutes apportioned lesson plans. I have no idea how I am going to squeeze in the work I promised I would deliver. I also have no idea what I will feed them for lunch – as once again we have run out of bread and the Against All Odds Girl will only eat bread and chocolate spread, as you know, and I am too tired to argue. The washing pile is building up and I know that the bathroom really could do with a clean. I should also check in with my over-70 parents and parents-in-law and I promised the girls we would Zoom chat this evening, but I may now have to work while doing the ironing.

The Husband is upstairs, which is his new workstation because every other room is occupied by a child. My children's schools are delivering online lessons.

The Teenager needs reminding that the Easter holidays have now finished but, who knows, because it's a bit like

Christmas and we are counting the lockdown weeks rather than actual dates or days of the week. He is playing his cards well, knowing the time to commute from bed to PC buys him further time in bed. Still, I must ask him if he is ready for the 9.30am login with anything resembling a schoolbook close to hand and perhaps he ought to brush his teeth, too. When he appears at the allotted time I am a little put out because we were promised lessons until 3pm, with a break for lunch, but his lovely tutor felt they could do with a 30-minute break to ease them in because, after all, they have had the most hectic of Easters.

I have no idea what to do with the other two, because the staff are on 'inset' days until Wednesday; I assume said staff are practising recording their own voices and uploading Twinkl worksheets. We decide to enter the PE with Joe T-shirt competition. The Against All Odds Girl has a spare white T-shirt and starts flicking her hair in a creative nod to excitement. She gets out the Sharpie pens and starts drawing cartoons of Joe Wicks and a globe of the world – it's only when she lifts the T-shirt that I realise the Sharpie has seeped into our oak kitchen table. I am scrubbing this out while muting the WhatsApp notifications and wondering where the Middle Child has gone. I had started to ask him about the book he was reading, *Goodnight Mister Tom,* but he has disappeared. He is found in his room, skulking around with his phone and a finger pressed down on YouTube. I give up on the novel comprehension, replacing it with an argument on screen time, knowing that I won't win. I decide it is time for a break, just as the Teenager appears and declares it is lunchtime. I Google 'removing Sharpie pens from surfaces' and 'how to homeschool' – hoping that you can get a bitesize answer to each. I look at my watch and it is only midday. I think it is going well, so far 😉.

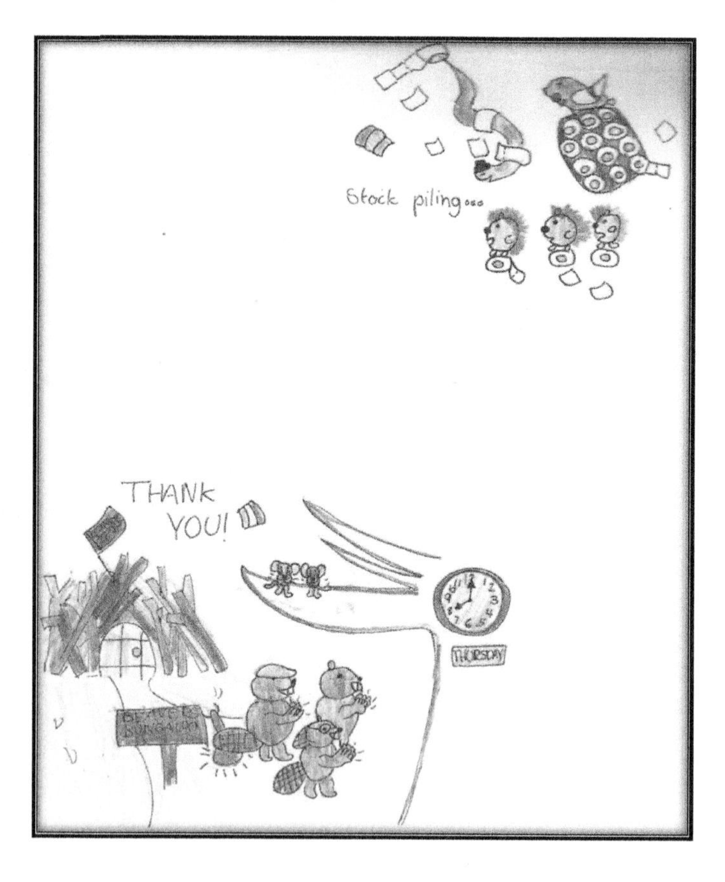

Panic buying – Tabitha Peters, aged 12

22 April, 2020 – Getting Wings

The United Kingdom has confirmed 763 new deaths, bringing the death toll to 18,100. The number of cases has reached 133,495. Foreign Secretary Dominic Raab has also confirmed the deaths of 69 National Health Service personnel as a result of the coronavirus pandemic.

In a Commons statement, Health Secretary Matt Hancock tells MPs 'we are at the peak' of the outbreak, but social distancing measures cannot be relaxed until the government's five tests have been met.

(Wikipedia, 2020)

School number two has launched its attack on us. They have gone for an uploading of work option – the idea is that the parents spend half of their working day trying to work out how to login and then find the appropriate worksheets. We then spend the rest of the allocated hours negotiating with our little darlings to do the work, which we either print out half a rainforest for them to fill in, or navigate our way around the IT to do it online and upload it before it disappears into the ether. The teacher then comments something witty or, if on a more serious note, adds some teaching point to justify the whole process as 'school' albeit 'not as we know it'.

The Against All Odds Girl appears at 7am by my bedside and physically prises my eyelids open. She wants it all to kick-off, but I know her well and the anticipation of 'online school' is akin to the passing excitement of pretty much anything that is new. I remember when we started piano lessons and she was psyched up three days before the half-hour event occurred. I had visions that this was it, we were going to be performing in teatime concerts and giving Mozart a run for his money, only to be disappointed that it was another flash in the pan. I now had a sizeable keyboard to use as an ironing station. Now this is the something new, except it's not a wedding and we don't need good luck, we need wine and for someone to remove the sledgehammer that looks enticing before it goes through the PC monitor.

We start with Greek mythology – you know the one about the boy who flies too close to the sun and his wax wings burn. The Against All Odds Girl must read this aloud with expression, which she translates as shouting and wild gesticulation. She has been watching too much of Piers Morgan on *Good Morning Britain.* The Husband, who is upstairs because every room in the house is filled with a child, starts thumping on the floor. I try to mute the Against All Odds Girl but she continues to be melodramatic. It would have been quite impressive if she could pronounce 'Icarus', but it comes out as if she has drunk a keg of cider and inhaled a pork pie. I keep repeating the name and it starts spinning around in my head like a wasp caught in a jar, jostling for head time with the thought on how long I can legitimately keep the bed sheets on without changing them and whether

Alan the postman changes his gloves at every house or just after every shift. It's busy in there.

The Middle Child arrives just as the Against All Odds Girl does a final bow. She is expecting an applause; he looks appropriately unimpressed and asks what I know about *Private Peaceful*, his Michael Morpurgo novel. He is comparing the various qualities of two competing front covers. The Against All Odds Girl is not impressed that her one-on-one is being interrupted, as she is under the impression that I am a personal teaching assistant, although she has made it clear that I am not the teacher because I am not qualified and therefore on a much lower band. I am wondering what the learning point is, in this current pandemic, of a boy that flies out of his tower in order to escape a king's entrapment and a half-man, half-bull creature – is it about how we all need to bear with imprisonment against things we can't always see or understand? Will my Year 3 child start assembling pigeon feathers and burning down candles to mesh it all together and jump out of her window? I am hoping she'll be sensible and start looking at Rapunzel and grow her hair as an option against the closure of all flights and the need to self-build flying machines.

The Middle Child wants me to do his work. He plays the card of not understanding, even though I know he can wax lyrical on YouTube to compare Match Attax cards for hours, so what's the difference? I wonder if the teacher will notice if I write it for him because quite frankly, I just want to get it done. Although I probably should check the Against All Odds Girl is not strapping feathers to her arms.

The Teenager says once again he has an empty half hour and asks if he can use it wisely by going on the Xbox. It's 9.30am and even I, who have massively lowered parental expectations, feel this is inappropriate. He laughs when I suggest a book; perhaps the story of Icarus, I say. This could help with his classics. He guffaws in disgust while telling me that anyone that makes homemade wings is not worth reading about and turns the Xbox on.

The Middle Child chooses maths next. I don't know how to find the area of a trapezium. Should I fess up to him that I have scraped through four decades without this knowledge quite well so far? The Against All Odds Girl is deciding to do art – that's not even on the online learning portal but she says she can send it to her teacher and hopefully will get a 'star'. I wonder if the parents will also get rewards, at the moment I'll take anything. She takes the paint brushes outside and an art easel that she forced me to buy, in a weak moment, of which there are many. She starts painting the garden and swings but decides after three attempts and another ream of paper that she can't make the swings the right size, they are too fat apparently. I try to weave in a lesson on adjectives and suggest other synonyms, feeling smug at my cross-lateral teaching. She says, 'massive'. We settle on, 'chubby', while glancing at my stomach.

There's some work on Roman roads but it's basically asking you to spend all afternoon looking at different websites and repeat episodes of *Horrible Histories* and I can't be bothered. I wonder if I can delete it from the online portal. It has now come to the point in the day when I am gathering birds' feathers and throwing them in the bin while researching how to erase teachers' work.

The Husband is telling the children they must stop printing things in colour because we will go bankrupt. He has a point. I WhatsApp him so the children can't hear and suggest breaking the printer deliberately, to save costs.

It's hot, hot enough to melt Icarus's wings so we decide to do some netball – the Against All Odds Girl drags the post up to the trampoline because she is frustrated that it can't be lowered, and she likes to win. The paints are drying up in the sun and there is kitchen paper flying around the garden because she was using it to blot with. The Middle Child is eating crisps in secret and hoping I won't notice, and the Teenager is dropping facts about how much of the earth is made up of water. This is a deliberate ploy to put me off the scent of some of the online gaming that is going on.

I declare the school day closed and raid the biscuit cupboard. It's empty. The crisps have all gone, too. Luckily there is a god because the wine fridge is stocked, and I decide it's teacher's reward time because, sadly, I didn't get a star today. So, some rocket fuel will have to do.

Violet Ground Beetle – Oli Manson, aged 6

24 April, 2020 – Zoom Armageddon

In the United Kingdom, hospitals in England report 587 deaths, bringing the death toll to 17,373.

A version of 'You'll Never Walk Alone', recorded by Captain Tom Moore and Michael Ball to raise money for the NHS Charities Together fund, reaches number one in the UK Singles Chart.

(Wikipedia, 2020)

The Against All Odds Girl and the Middle Child have class calls scheduled at the same time. We have only just got over the incident of the saxophone when the Teenager spent half of the allocated call switching the mics around and I could see the teacher picking his nose in boredom. I cross-check the times, hoping there has been a mistake – surely the school wouldn't ask us to be on call for two children at the same time? I chat with the other mums and it is correct. It's 1.59pm and I have a knot forming in my stomach as I wonder how I can run incognito between the two to fix audio sound and provide seamless passwords. The Middle Child kicks off and waves his hands at me to shoo me away; apparently, I am no longer required, my role as home educator has come to an end now that a 'real teacher' is back on the scene. We are left hanging for the Against All Odds Girl's chat to start – we take out another laptop (we are collecting them) and wonder if it's our inept tech or that the teacher is on a bike ride.

The WhatsApp group goes wild and we ricochet between abandoning the school ship and going it alone in our own Zoom call – after all, we have now got our homeschooling badge so we can do anything, right? The Middle Child is lost deep in conversation about pet carnage and how many 'imerits' they have all got – I am assuming he hasn't got many, based on the last post he made online, in which he told the teacher that he couldn't complete the work on prime number puzzles because he didn't know and his parents couldn't work it out, either.

The Against All Odds Girl is squealing for a colourful background. I try to slide my fingers across the laptop, while ducking my head under the table so as not to be seen. My back is going into some sort of spasm but still I feel it is worth it for her to be seen on Golden Gate Bridge and not in north Essex. The call comes to an end as they have run out of pets to FaceTime and they agree to dial in at the same time next week. The Middle Child does the same – by next Friday I vow to find my doppelganger sister so we can 'scene set' the Big Apple and Phuket as backgrounds at 2pm.

The Teenager is on Latin.

Question 8: omnes bibebant et ridebant (1 point):

- Everyone was eating and drinking
- Everyone was drinking and smiling

- Everyone was eating and smiling

- Everyone was drinking and celebrating

I sardonically suggest that it can only be the first, 'everyone was eating and drinking' because no one would be smiling or celebrating until the kids go back to school.

I feel we need to do something nurturing; I reach out to the local Facebook group with a request for tadpoles - I feel momentarily virtuous, slipping out of my slummy mummy shoes for a quick flirtation with impressive parenting. I explain that the darlings would ooh and aah to see the transformation into frogs and it would provide a great nature lesson. I get two responses: the first says she would have helped but her dog has spent the best part of the last few days shovelling frogspawn down like caviar; the other throws the book at me and says it is illegal to move tadpoles from their natural habitat, under the Wildlife and Countryside Act, 1981. I decide to leave the group and ditch my responsibilities to lost local cats and defibrillation meetings in the village hall because I fear being put in prison. I return to the cosy familiarity that is provided by TikTok, realising that 'good parenting' is clearly illegal.

We still have some work to do. I try to revisit the idea of the Roman Road project to the Against All Odds Girl, in which we are supposed to research facts and complete a worksheet. She flicks her hair and says, 'I don't care about those roads, I only care about these roads.' That shuts that idea down and, based on the fact that earlier we had to part with four eclairs to complete a column addition worksheet, I feel we may have to let this one go because I have run out of chocolate and my back still hurts from the Zooming.

It's 3.30pm and I feel the weekend should start. I slink off for a cup of tea but the Middle Child asks if I will play badminton on the basis that the Against All Odds Girl is 'rubbish' at it and the Teenager is asleep or 'omnes bibebant et ridebant'. I reluctantly agree because I can't provide tadpoles as entertainment and the Zoom calls have dried up. We can only find one shuttlecock, which appears to be half-eaten, even though we don't have a dog or any of the pets that the children's friends have been showing off on FaceTime. We make do with the oddly-spinning object, which the Middle Child accepts because he is now used to things that are massively sub-standard. I vow that next week I will have perfectly-sized shuttlecocks, the doppelganger will have arrived, and we will have purchased some sort of pet or be in prison for trying to acquire one.

Stay apart – Tabitha Peters, aged 12

27 April, 2020 – Chickens Aren't Just for Lockdown

The United Kingdom has reported 413 new deaths, bringing the death toll to 20,732, and has reported 4,463 new cases, bringing the total to 152,840.

In his first public statement since returning to work, Boris Johnson says the UK is 'at the moment of maximum risk' but 'we are now beginning to turn the tide' as he urges people not to lose patience with the restrictions.

(Wikipedia, 2020)

It's Monday. The worksheet says, 'Week 2, Day 1'. It feels more like 'Month 12, Day 31' although I know for a fact that it's not New Year's Eve, which is a sadness because the thought of zooming ahead to 2021 and forgetting that 2020 ever happened is appealing. It's also week six of the lockdown and week six of children being at home and homeschooled. For most families a period of this length would mark the end of the long summer holidays but this is a case of Easter, summer and then summer again being thrown at us with no warning or playdates on the horizon.

The Against All Odds Girl is confronted with some work on adverbs. We have printed out five sheets on this, which is progress from last week when we were overzealous with the printing button and parted with 25 copies of Perseus and a woman with snakes on her head, or as the children refer to Medusa, 'Mummy when she is homeschooling'.

We are cost-saving, so the printing is in black and white. The worksheet asks you to highlight and categorise the adverbs into 'how, when and where' by underlining in different colours. The monochrome is obscuring which colours should go with which category. I temporarily curse expensive printer cartridges and taking social distancing measures to the extreme by going running on my own more often because I am now hobbling from two days of 8k runs and the time it takes to walk to the PC to cross-check palette options has now doubled. I also need to source the correct coloured crayons, which should be straightforward but none of them have leads in or are in their box. The search takes a further 15 minutes, with another five for repeated sharpenings and location of sharpeners, some of which appear not to fit the crayons, defying the myth that one size fits all is actually true. Perhaps that only applies if you have invested in Smiggle pencils or Smencils, which the Against All Odds Girl says is a requirement for the classroom.

I make a note to go to the children's beds first, when trying to locate coloured crayons for English grammar. We take in the learning notes about not all adverbs ending in 'ly'. The Against All Odds Girl does not like the myriad exceptions and takes a dislike to those that express time, place or manner. She says that if you have rules they should apply, so we will only consider 'carefully', 'excitedly' and 'loudly' as options. I will remind her that she has championed regulations and their adherence when it comes to bedtime tonight.

The Middle Child is analysing a chapter of *Private Peaceful* and the main character's feelings towards an older girl. I try to explain that boys may feel differently towards girls when they are 16, as opposed to 11. He looks at me quizzically, wondering if this is another blow akin to the realities of the Tooth Fairy and Father Christmas. The Against All Odds Girl interrupts with questions on how 'frog jumping' can help with subtraction. She feels it is of little help and uses some head shaking to make this known. Since we failed to source the tadpoles for a brief visit with wholesomeness, I feel that amphibians are not our friend when it comes to learning. She ditches the worksheets and decides to draw a picture of a girl with an umbrella standing under a rain cloud and a further one of a child looking at the Eiffel Tower. I feel this 'off piste' moment has covered both weather changes and geography, as well as French. I thank her for this genius.

It's lunchtime and we take some time out to look at the chicken coop we have decided to build. The Husband has been binging on YouTube clips of chicken mansions. In these homesteads the chicken Meccas come with self-feed systems made from sewer pipes. I buy into the idea, imagining the little darlings collecting hen eggs and skipping down the garden comparing double-yoker stats. Yet in reality, I can't help but wonder if the show and tell chicken lovers on YouTube aren't permanent self-isolators, as none appear to be in visual shot of neighbours or must go to work, like ever. I worry that this latest project may therefore just be a lockdown obsession and that it will be similar to when Christmas is over and you have to pack the novelty Santa jumpers away, except this time we are left with too many hybrids enraged that their self-feeder sewer pipe has a hole in it. Still, we go with it and the Against All Odds Girl fully embraces the notion. Anything to get away from 'frog' calculations.

We decide to convert the children's treehouse into the chicken palace in a nod to recycling, although having invested many hours that have now put a dent in the homeschooling schedule we may as well have received a nice flat pack. The Against All Odds Girl and I start to empty the treehouse of detritus past - amongst the treasures are some science goggles and an overdue school library book. I wonder now if the lichen-laden play den has been depleting the NHS of its much-needed PPE and if you can pay 365 x 3 overdue days of late library book fees in sub-standard eggs or pencil sketches of the Eiffel Tower.

It's at the point that we choose names for the hens that I know that there is no backing out. Mine is Margot, so that I can 'upmarket' the whole experience and block out the thought that the chickens will be feeding from pipes produced for disposing of human faeces.

It's time to return, briefly, to some schoolwork and the Husband says he needs to go to a meeting, which is 'up the stairs and turn right'. I, meanwhile, am delighted to spend the afternoon watching the science teacher explain what permeable means and how absorption differs between stones. It's a 26-minute video and the earlier 'head on table' which I scolded the Teenager for is now looking rather hypocritical. So far today I have read chapter three of the Middle Child's Michael Morpurgo novel and learnt that slate is impermeable and, indeed, how to spell that. The Teenager is delighted to tell me that there was a time when Tesco burgers were 29% horsemeat. This is senior school 'science'. His interest is counteracted by horror when I tell him that I remember the scandal and we probably consumed quite a few.

It's 4.34pm and the Against All Odds Girl still has spellings and times tables to learn, there's sax and piano to cross off the list to boot but my client is probably not interested in the excuse about too much homework and would like a newsletter delivered, as agreed. I start work at 4.35pm and wonder if the pandemic is capable of stopping time, too, because I need some *Back to the Future* magic to reverse the hours, so I can step off the hamster wheel for a while. Actually, I am not fussed about which movie because *Cinderella* also has its merits, as the house could do with a good scrub.

Brambling – Oli Manson, aged 6

30 April, 2020 – No Screens Day and Other Things

The United Kingdom has reported 674 deaths, bringing the death toll to 26,711. Authorities in England have reported 391 new deaths, bringing the hospital death toll there to 20,137.

Prime Minister Boris Johnson says the UK is 'past the peak' of the COVID-19 outbreak but that the country must not 'risk a second spike' and announces that he will set out a 'comprehensive plan' for easing the lockdown 'next week'. He also stresses the importance of keeping down the reproductive rate, which 'is going to be absolutely vital to our recovery'.

Captain Tom Moore celebrates his 100th birthday and is made an honorary colonel by the Queen. His appeal to raise money for the NHS reaches £32m.

(Wikipedia, 2020)

The Against All Odds Girl has written a story about a dog eating loo roll. I try to explain that this is now a hard-to-come-by commodity and perhaps she ought to consider a different item for the animal to chew. She says she won't change her mind because on our last trip to Sainsbury's they did sell it. She continues with her narrative about a wild four-legged creature called, 'Boof-head', and its owner, 'Princess'. I wonder how many adults with first names that are royal titles, own dogs that have long vowel sounds as part of their name and suggest they are continuously fighting. But anything goes in these lockdown times and this is English, and the purpose is dialogue writing. The task says, maximum one hour, but I don't think the teacher has allocated enough time for the hot chocolate requests, uploading and printing out or the discussions on the price of the aforesaid lavatory paper or how indeed it is made – fibre and water, if you are asking. There is also the 'off piste' moment when she decides she doesn't want to do this anymore as she feels she has done enough for one day, although at this point it is 9.30am and we have only written two sentences, one of which is about eating 'chewnar' – which I wrongly believe is a moment of genius because 'tuna' is on the weekly spelling list, before realising that we obviously need to spend some time learning that one, too.

The online portal continues to flash at me and there is still the work on Roman Roads to do, plus a new activity, which adds to the first one that we haven't done either. The worksheet on rocks is winking at me as well but since we have spent half an hour creating text boxes for the writing to go into I am pretty sure that once again we can write that one off because the Against All Odds Girl has got so wound up about it she has shooed me away and decided that the Teenager would be a better source of help. They start to speak to each other over headphones and I can hear 'for roofs' being boomed across the airways together with, 'Tell her [that's me] you don't have to do it for another week.' The conspiracy of deadlines continues.

The Teenager hasn't got much time, however, to rescue his little sister from rock categorisation because he has science and today's task is to build a model of DNA to recall its structure and function. The teacher asks them to use sweets to do this. One boy on the chat board posts, 'Sir, if I don't do well, I now know that the mint Aeros are extremely explosive when chopped in half by a ruler.' Another adds, 'Sir, my dad has gone to buy marshmallows.' The Teenager asks if we have any Wine Gums; I admit to him that his brother has eaten them all. He then asks if we have pasta tubes. I inform him that if we had pasta it would most certainly have been eaten and wouldn't be permitted for the use of science experiments. He reaches for the Lego as another friend comments, 'I tried to build my model, but it just looked like a ladder.' I think the teacher may have left the lesson at this point.

We spend the next part of the day constructing a picture of different layers in bright colours, like a Matisse. I explain this is in direct juxtaposition to my mood, which is nudging towards the darker colours. The Against All Odds Girl decides to collect items of nature from the garden in her welly boots as inspiration for the collage before proceeding to cut up tiny, I mean really tiny, pieces of paper and then gluing half of them to the piece of paper and the oak table, which has only just recovered from the Sharpie pens incident. We then get even more upset because we can't work out the scanner to 'show and tell' the masterpiece to her class via Zoom, so compromise on a wall display in the kitchen, which should be straightforward if we could find the Blu Tack stash. Instead, we must peel off artwork of old and negotiate which picture will be depleted of enough Blu Tack to keep it stuck to the wall of fame.

I'm feeling a little aggrieved generally because a friend invited me to join a Facebook group called Family Lockdown Tips and Ideas. This means that I am bombarded several times a day by the one million plus members with their perfect parenting, ranging from the themed evenings they host with their smiling families to a DIY escape room (I mean seriously), a homemade arcade with prizes and giveaways and nightly renditions of ballads and suppers cooked by delighted teenagers. In contrast, my children's screen time seems to have spiked in a mirroring exercise with the coronavirus curve and the height of the Shard no longer looks impressive. In none of these posts are there bored children in front of devices or youngsters refusing to go out on daily bike rides.

I tell the darlings that we must have a no-screen day and play Boggle, sing songs and make elderflower cordial. Wailing ensues and some, 'Are you serious?' comments. 'Yes,' I say, 'Because it will be fun.' 'I'll do it too,' I add, although I don't really mean this, you can't really expect me not to look at my phone all day because I need to check in with the Family Lockdown group and see who has also painted their front door in rainbow colours or dressed up as a flamenco dancer and created original, choreographed set pieces.

By 4pm the Teenager is muttering under his breath that life as you know it is over and what sane parent actually does this and why should he read around the subject or play his saxophone piece, which should have been a signal in itself that screen time had got too much as his teacher confirms that he has chosen, 'Phone It In' Fortnite emote. The Middle Child is playing it cool. He declares dinner an absolute sensation and offers his help in clearing it away. This is in direct contrast to the day before, or the day before that one or, indeed, ever. He then asks if we can play the Capital City game: The Netherlands, Amsterdam; Peru, Lima; Kenya, Nairobi; Canada, Ottawa' – he plants the countries deliberately to boost his ratings as compliant child number one. I feel this is a tactic to get the screen time back and I also realise this could go on too long and I am dying to look at my phone.

Perhaps I could nip off to the loo, where hopefully no pet has untangled the Sainsbury's treasures because then I could have a quick look to see what the Family Lookdown group is doing and take a deep breath before I get out there and construct a DIY anything. I suggest we play Risk, the game where you win by occupying neighbouring countries. 'But you're not allowed to travel, Mum, haven't you seen the news?' asks the Against All Odds Girl and the boys nod in a 'well, she's right' kind of a way. I've just read about a couple in Mississippi who have converted a Boeing 727 into a three bedroom home complete with hot tub and I feel that perhaps everything is grounded, after all.

Next, I suggest Monopoly, but the Middle Child argues that the economy is collapsing, and you can't get a mortgage easily so there's no point buying up Mayfair or Park Lane. 'How about, Guess Who?' I say cheerily but the Teenager reminds me that we had to abandon that last time because the Husband introduced the possibility of asking if anyone had facial hair and that included half the suspects so that one was out. It's too late to ask anyone to dress up in ski wear or figures from popular history so I suggest a movie. 'But that's a screen,' says the Against All Odds Girl. 'Well, I've changed the rules,' I reply, and we settle down to *Johnny English.* While they are still and quiet, I delete all restrictions to screens and leave the Family Lockdown Tips and Ideas group.

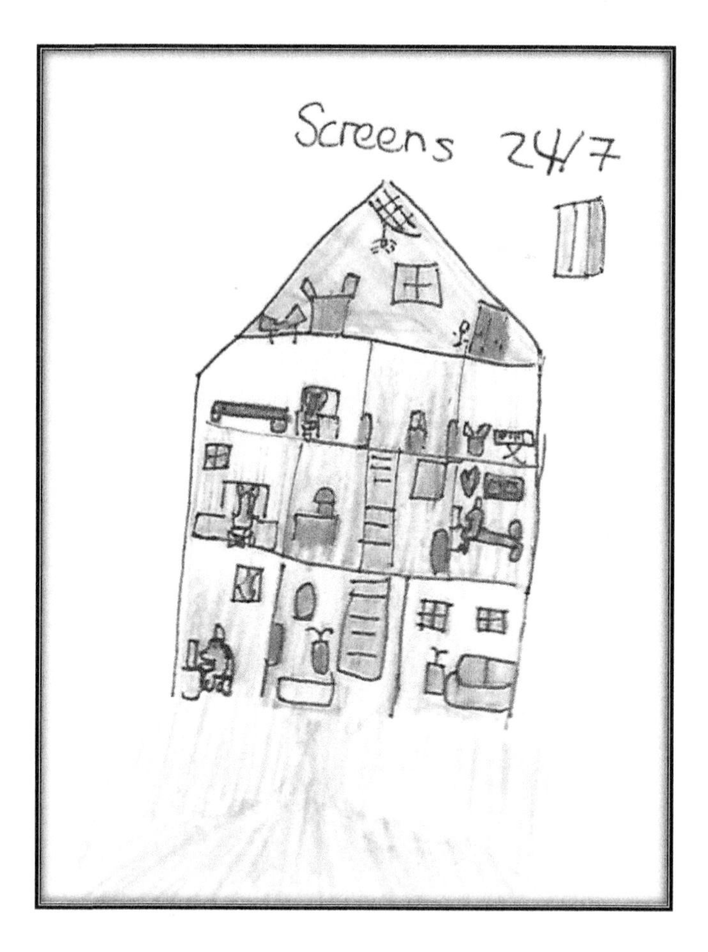

Spiking screen times – Tabitha Peters, aged 12

MAY, 2020

4 May, 2020 – Nail Tales and Fraction Frenzies

The United Kingdom has reported 288 deaths, bringing the death toll to 28,734.

Apple and Google approve a test version of the NHS tracing app.

(Wikipedia, 2020)

I'm measuring the weeks according to the gel polish left on my fingers. A quarter on two fingers is hanging on in there. A rudimentary calculation based upon the average tenure being a fortnight means I am doing well. It must be at least week seven, which it is. Their stubbornness surely defies all odds, which at the same time I salute as a reminder of the life we had before lockdown, when nails were worth being painted for.

It's Monday, not that this means anything these days and it's a notion that the children are also living and breathing. The Teenager is still in bed at 8.54am and I know that his tutor is expecting him to be online and registered by 9am. I tell him, or rather yell at him, that he ought to get up. He has perfected the sub-five-minute change with eyes still closed. He throws on the clothes that are conveniently still at the foot of his bed from the night before and yawns his way down the stairs to his desk. He mouths at me, 'bacon sandwich,' and flicks on the screen to be greeted by a smiling teacher, who in contrast is obviously up and dressed and waxing lyrical about timetables and focus. I slip the bacon sandwich into his lap and he gives me a thumbs up. I'm not sure if this is for me or for himself, because he is obviously delighted that he has clocked another long sleep and dodged a telling off from the school and us by fulfilling the requirement of registration on time and therefore also all parental expectations concerning presenteeism.

I turn my attentions to the other two. The Against All Odds Girl is looking at equivalent fractions. After some huffing and puffing when confronted with the learning sheets I decide we should go down the practical path. We're out of chocolate, which is no surprise, but fully stocked on apples, which relates to a dodging of the good stuff and an overstuffing of the bad ones. I begin by demonstrating a half, a quarter, then eighths, except I haven't cut the apple straight and so a half is more like two thirds and one third, and five of the eighths is more like six or seven. The Against All Odds Girl looks at me quizzically and suggests that if they are equal then the Pope is also no longer Catholic. My fraction lesson is rejected, and she returns to the neat fraction wall that the teacher has given her, declaring that, after all, she does understand it because wonky apple slices demonstrate nothing but an inept apple corer and another sub-standard 'parent stand-in' teaching lesson. The apple is also a little brown, or beige if we are being polite, so it is doubly rejected as both a maths lesson and a healthy snack.

We move on. The Middle Child is writing a character letter from the position of 'empathy' to another character within *Private Peaceful.* I explain that empathy means standing in someone else's shoes and understanding how they may feel. He says he sees. 'Is it a bit like how I can see that you hate homeschooling because we ask you to do most of it and the printer never works?' he asks. 'Yes,' I say, thinking that this must be the best lesson in the day because surely that denotes a shred of sympathy for my position, although, his detachment from the printer anxiety and the uploading and downloading involved in the online lesson obviously hasn't attracted the proportional empathy I would expect because he is now sitting on his behind looking at his 139 message alerts from 'Da Boys' or the 'Roboxlians'.

Next, I am torn between science, which is another video sensation on rocks – although there is a promise of a volcano erupting, which may brighten things up - and the sock pile, which is also groaning. I decide I need to go down the Montessori route and teach life-skills while we're on about basalt and magma. I set up the learning rocks video on my phone and prop it up against the sock basket, which looks like Earth's crust about to blow. There are piles of school socks to pair, although I wonder if this is a pointless exercise, like the fractions lesson, because, after all, there aren't any socks being worn, particularly school ones. The Against All Odds Girl pitches in with some pairing – 'two make a whole,' she says. I am aglow with cross-lateral fraction teaching, although I say 100 makes too many socks and a hundredth of anything is too small a fraction to be concerned with. We drop half of them on the floor, continuing to miss vital rock elements, which we later regret when the Against All Odds Girl must fill out the worksheet and Google can't find the answers. This means we must re-start the video and watch it while not pairing socks, making cottage pie, or answering WhatsApp messages about the possibility of schools re-opening on 1 June, as I try to dampen down a beaming smile. The children ask why I am so happy because this is an oddity, when it's mainly been scowling and frowning since school closures began. I don't answer, concentrating instead on a volcanic eruption for the second time.

Everyone is a little scratchy, which means it's time for the 4pm bike ride, the usual peak of the daily fallout. We've been talking about VE Day as we pedal. The Middle Child and the Against All Odds Girl want to know about the Blitz in London. I tell them about how children in World War Two were often evacuated to the countryside to live with people they may not have known. This comes as something of a horror to the Against All Odds Girl, who says that sounds even worse than having to be homeschooled by your mother during the pandemic. I try to explain that really, we haven't got it so bad because all we have do is stay at home until it is safe, and the virus is under control. I can see her thinking, which is an interesting sight as there is a slight upward lift in her bicycle helmet as she does so. She says that the children in World War Two went to school but in comparison she has to stay home, so I am wrong. They had it better because at least they got taught by qualified teachers whereas she and her brothers have to put up with me, who tries to wing it in maths with rotten apples and considers sock-pairing to be a viable substitute for science.

The school day closes as we brake to a halt in the driveway and I get ready for my Zoom chat with my friends. We have agreed to wear dangly earrings to make it 'fun' because I need to practise smiling and at least if everyone is looking at my ears, they won't notice that I have gel nails hanging on at the tips of two fingers. This serves as a further blessing because I have just been asked to edit a book by a client but am hoping we can dodge Zoom chats or FaceTime calls to discuss it because I don't want my barely-there rouge-tipped nails to be seen. Although, at least I have some socks, so perhaps I can pose with my feet up on the desk but with my fingers behind my back. Knowing my luck, I'll fall off the chair and the client will get some holey socks in their face and a one-fingered, red-tipped bird up at the screen.

It never rains but it pours – the Against All Odds Girl, aged 8

6 May, 2020 – Groundhog Day on Speed

The United Kingdom has reported 539 new deaths, bringing the death toll to 30,615. (7 May, 2020.)

At his first Prime Minister's Questions since returning to work Boris Johnson says he 'bitterly regrets' the crisis in care homes and is 'working very hard' to tackle it. Johnson also pledges to reach a target of 200,000 daily UK coronavirus tests by the end of May.

(Wikipedia, 2020)

I think that Bill Murray had it good in his version of Groundhog Day because the whole thing lasts 101 minutes and at least he gets to see people. Our version lacks the excitement of a rodent signalling spring; it's just schoolwork with the expectation that it will be worse the following day because you failed to complete the tasks on the day before that and the day before that one and the daffodils have now died. I'd say the reality is more of a special measures St Trinian's that is caught on a continuous time-loop, yet sadly you can't give in your notice and go to the better school down the road, like ever.

We've had tears today and that's not just been from me. The Against All Odds Girl was given the task of re-writing Roald Dahl's *Fantastic Mr Fox* using a substitute animal or family of animals and twisting the thin, fat and short farmers into something or things similar but also unique. The creativity went into overdrive and she went through various species, thankfully none picked from a wet market in Wuhan, yet cross-referenced with some possibles from the geography exercise to document animals from the tundra. At one point we did have the concept of a snowy owl stealing food from various-sized lady farmers, because the Against All Odds Girl wanted to promote the role of females in rural areas, while acknowledging that Slimming World was on the agenda for most of them. It is now 11am and she hasn't written one word because we have spent most of the morning deciding on the relative merits of each animal, further time being clocked up with the attempts to choose an animal with a witty alliterative title – 'Owl Oddities' or 'Rascal Rabbits'. The next step is to write a 'story mountain', although at this point, I feel we have already ascended a real mountain and the story is that it is exhausting, and we are losing the will to live.

Some arrows and boxes with illustrations of plump middle-aged ladies and hooting owls with feathery wings follow, with few words bar 'fat' 'thin' and 'medium'. She has been looking at my 'Lose It!' tracker app too much because she suggests that they should ditch the 'bread' while announcing that she needs a break and asks if we can clean out the fish tank. I say to her that she really needs to crack on with the English and there is some more fraction work to do, too. She bats some eyelashes at me and promises that she will, although I have become immune to these vows and should know a whole lot better than to believe that this is true. Despite this we press ahead like the politicians and start to clean out Spotty and Dotty's tanks (we're into rhyming as well as alliteration). The Against All Odds Girl remarks that she would like to be a fish because they happily swim around their tank knowing nothing about lockdown or COVID-19.

There's a double concern here about the number of animals she would like to be, as well as the worry that she would rather be in a Groundhog Day like the goldfish and us, infinitum. The fish are put back in their clean home, wide-eyed at the lack of algae and agog with newness. Still no words are written but all the animals have been considered and the fish are happy.

In contrast the Middle Child has worked out that if he does everything at high speed this means that he can have most of the afternoon off, every afternoon. He's on Groundhog Day at high speed. He also got the message about bed-making because he knows that the Q&A back and forth on that one every morning, 'have you, or haven't you?' is A. boring and B. another timewaster. Compliance on speed, however, does come with some pitfalls because the Against All Odds Girl is on go-slow and the Teenager is still in online lessons, albeit with his head on his desk. This leaves the Middle Child with no playmates other than the fish, who are more interested in seeing out of the tank for the first time in a few weeks, and I have no time to entertain, so suggest to him that he hangs up the washing for me. Tomorrow, I fear, he may not be so keen to flatten out his duvet and hide his dressing gown under his pillow.

The Teenager has perfected another bed-to-desk sub-five-minute manoeuvre and has done the habitual wink and thumbs up for a bacon sandwich to appear in his lap, while he grapples with gradients and equations. I wouldn't have blamed the teacher for a total meltdown judged on the student comments in the chat box, ranging from a total wipeout of understanding to downright laziness: 'Sir, how do you do 3C?'; another puts, 'I couldn't see the screen sorry,'; and someone else, 'I don't get 3A.' The teacher dutifully comments, 'Put the 'x' values into the equation y=2x+2 to find the y values.' A student writes back, 'Yep,' and with that the lesson is concluded.

I squeeze in a bit of social media because I need some escapism. Facebook is feeding me an advert from Ordnance Survey for maps that I can download and colour in. I am wondering if someone failed to tell them that it's a little torturous to look at maps of places that you have zero chance of going to anywhere soon, coupled with a homeschooling schedule that means leisure times are filled with sharpening crayons and then sitting with your little darlings, who have had you and them in tears for the best part of the day. If it was Tinder, I would have swiped left on that one (and, for the record, I had to look that up!). I am at a loss as to why I am not getting ads for vats of wine because that would be a winner at this point, even though it is only midday.

The Husband is still building the chicken coop. It has been a few weeks now and marked by the fact that no one now asks how it's going because they have detected some low-level grumbling in my voice, and I can't disguise it anymore. It is big and getting bigger and I am wondering if it is for hybrids or the three children. They have been a little noisy and he has had to seal up the makeshift office door with a draught excluder to dampen down their squeals, which makes a change from the habitual stamping on the floor that is Morse code for 'shut up'. Still, I think that maybe it's not a bad thing because either the chickens are going to be upgraded to something of a palace or, if the lockdown doesn't end soon, we can move to stage three and put us or the children out there - but definitely not together.

Fox – Oli Manson, aged 6

11 May, 2020 – Half Measures and Morticia Haircuts

The United Kingdom has reported 269 deaths, bringing the national death toll to 31,855. (10 May, 2020)

The UK government publishes a 50-page document setting out further details of the phases for lifting the lockdown restrictions. Boris Johnson gives more details as he makes his first statement on the virus to Parliament.

Amid concerns about the safety of people returning to work, Johnson tells the Downing Street daily briefing he is not expecting a 'sudden big flood' of people returning to work, and that companies will have to prove they have introduced safety measures before they can reopen.

The UK government advises people in England to wear face coverings in enclosed spaces where social distancing is not possible, such as on public transport and in shops.

(Wikipedia, 2020)

It's Christmas, according to our maths teacher. The Against All Odds Girl is multiplying and dividing by 10 and 100 and sticking the answers onto a print out of a festive tree, although in this version there are no baubles or tinsel and therefore it feels like we are the last to get in on the invitation and this is the only tree left in the shop. We have had to shape 30 triangles with the sums on and stick them in according to the right answers. Half of them have fallen on the floor so we repeat the process, cutting out and sticking in, not to mention lifting off the paper because we stuck the wrong bits in the wrong places and one ended up on the Against All Odds Girl's bottom, possibly when she took her tenth break of the morning to consume a Wagon Wheel at high speed.

Still, it was welcome respite from the hilarity of the planets work in which she chose to fact-file about Uranus, much to the Teenager's amusement, whose quips on the name result in the Against All Odds Girl physically beating him due to the upset over the teasing. It didn't help that he then pulled the triangle sticker with 2700 off her behind, ensuring some more repeated low-level eight-year-old aggression. Still, we were tickled that Uranus spins in the opposite way to the Earth and the other planets, as we champion oddity in this house because it makes us feel normal. The Against All Odds Girl announces she needs a bath. It's midday and who am I to argue as anything goes in the 'bizarrity' that is the time vacuum of lockdown and at least a hot soak means we are not cutting out equilateral shaped maths sums or trying to locate glue sticks that haven't dried up to attach them with.

The Teenager declares he has got 15 out of 30 on his maths test. He knows that I won't be happy with 50 per cent, so softens the blow with, 'The teacher says this was above the class average because it's a higher level.' I chew this over as a plausible explanation and accept that half of anything in the lockdown is currently OK and nod in affirmation, which now he feels he can get away with ad infinitum. Schools are going back on 1 June and that's not even at a 50 per cent level, which has been heralded as a positive step, so who am I to argue about the stats that signal winning. The Middle Child is certainly delighted about this because he falls into the Year 6 category and therefore can dutifully oblige to pitch up in his classroom. He announced some while ago that homeschool was tragic and he really prefers proper teachers and real-life friends, as opposed to the ones he seems currently obsessed with down a WhatsApp chat group or hanging in a TikTok video. He also uploaded the maths to the English teacher and the English to the maths teacher so his ying and yang are at odds and he is in danger of flunking both classes.

The Against All Odds Girl declares between lessons that she wants her hair cut into a bob. It has been brewing for a while and with the midday bath it seems the right time to oblige. We can multi-task and consume a ham sandwich with the nearly off bread while we're at it. Having failed as a stand-in teacher I assume that trying it out as a hairdresser will be equally doomed. I therefore decide to go for it with a 'hold it all in one' ponytail and cut strategy, which works to an extent but then there is the tapering. So basically, the longer bits that get pulled into the bunch still end up longer. She looks a bit like Morticia Addams because she isn't very happy, and some scowling accompanies this. I blame it on the eating of the sandwich because it was at the point that she went for the double chew that the scissors went in. She escapes a buzz haircut but announces that I must pay double for the catastrophe to Colonel Tom and the NHS, amounting to at least £25, far more than we have ever paid for her hair to be cut previously. I am grappling with the idea that I am continuously punished for all the DIY – the homeschooling, the cooking and the hairdressing - and now I must pay for the disasters while getting the flack for them. I wonder if Rishi Sunak has a package for repayment of overpriced home haircuts and the mounting costs of schoolwork bribery.

I decide it's time to call it a day because I need to catch up on the latest instructions on going to work but staying at home and seeing a friend but social distancing and travelling to Scotland from north Essex for some daily exercise. Plus it's almost wine o'clock even though it's Monday but I declare it's #airportrulesinit during lockdown and I need some lady fuel to warm up to the idea of clearing up the hair from the floor, which is now mixed in with the triangle sums and the crumbs of stale half-and-half bread.

Friends are everything – Tabitha Peters, aged 12

19 May, 2020 – Impotence and the Periodic Table

In the United Kingdom, London's Metropolitan Police arrested 19 people breaking social distancing rules while protesting about the government's response to the pandemic, in Hyde Park. (16 May, 2020)

Figures from the Office for National Statistics show the number of people claiming Jobseeker's Allowance increased by 856,500 in April, to 2.1 million. In response to this, Chancellor Rishi Sunak says that it will take time for the UK economy to recover and it is 'not obvious there will be an immediate bounceback'.

Captain Tom Moore, who raised £32m for NHS charities, is to be knighted for his fundraising efforts, following a special nomination from Boris Johnson.

(Wikipedia, 2020)

The Against All Odds Girl is on 'ie' spellings. The instruction is to put, 'fields, chief, piece and brief' into sentences. She starts with, 'The fields are green and lush', which is an oddity because last time I looked there were dandelions growing on the grass and the brown patches were matching the green ones in a kind of salute to patchworks. Next it is, 'A piece of cake', which figures as every time I turn around, she is stuffing it down. This is followed by, 'Brief and quotient'. I would say this is a self-reflection of the amount of work she is doing as it is increasingly short and the result of division into smaller pieces as the days go by, although I had no idea that she knew the word 'quotient' and put that down to a clever mistake or a Google cut and paste exercise. The finale though is something not to forget – she ponders over what to do with 'chief'. The result is, 'The chief is impotent' – I look at her and she looks at me. She feels delighted that she has catapulted the big man into the realms of those that are important, while I feel that perhaps he needs to go out and buy some Viagra, if of course the other chiefs haven't bought it all up to get through the lockdown.

Next up is an emoji multiplication crossword. I am increasingly thinking that maths these days is not really about rows of sums but is a sort of fancy-dress parade. At the beginning of the week it was multiplying and dividing by sticking sums onto a Christmas tree and today it is times tables by happy and sad faces. Someone needs to get straight with the children and break the news that maths isn't art and craft in disguise but rows of boring sums with no festive bauble or smiley face pretending otherwise. The horrendous process of trying to get out of her the answer to 11 x 10 is further exasperated by the fact that she keeps leaning her elbow onto the laptop, re-starting the YouTube craft tutorial on how to make a bookmark of a panda. We are now repeating what the multiplication is and getting no responses because she is too busy looking dewy-eyed at the possibility of cutting and colouring an animal to stick into her book that she refuses to read. Still, we press on and after a lot of hideous tables repetition, plus muting of the distracting YouTube, we can reveal something of a Pac-Man type emoji with a tear drop on one side. I am glad that it feels the same as I do about the whole experience.

The Teenager announces he is writing to Waitrose about palm oil. This is geography and a youthful demonstration about sustainability. I tell him that he doesn't need to worry about speaking to up-market supermarkets because he is doing a very good job already about abstaining. After all, he hasn't washed his hair for about a week, and he has worn the same hoodie for close to a fortnight – doing his bit protesting about the palm oil in shampoo and laundry detergent. Job done.

It's Friday Zoom day with the classes and again they have sensibly organised a double whammy for both year groups with just half an hour apart. I am darting from room to room, putting in passwords for modern dance online for Year 6 and virtual coffee mornings for Year 3. The Against All Odds Girl is not impressed that she may have to spend an hour with some middle-aged mums drinking coffee and waxing lyrical about teenage washing habits, while the Middle Child refuses to put on a unitard and do a paradiddle tap dance. We eventually sort them, and everyone is Zoomed in on time and fake smiling. The Middle Child is doing a class quiz - one of the brainy kids asks what the chemical symbol of Tungsten is. The chat goes awfully quiet because most of them have been dumbed down for eight weeks and can only just about still write their name. They press on and everything is realigned when the next question is, 'Who has raised over £32 million for the NHS?' and everyone can answer that one.

The Against All Odds Girl appears to be at some sort of a bohemian online party where the children just lie around on their floor and say how bored they are to the class teacher. It doesn't go unnoticed that she is still in her pyjamas and it is now 2pm – the haircut from earlier in the week is starting to show up some defects so now she looks like one of the orphans out of *Annie*, which she dramatises when she says that she hasn't been out on a pony like everyone else or been reading anything other than the instructions of a sub-standard craft bookmark.

Still, it's the weekend and we are planning how far we can go for our multiple allowances of exercise. We are prepared to spend longer in the car then the actual exercise because no one said it had to be 'matchy matchy' and quite frankly at this point having them all strapped in and sitting still for any amount of time, preferably with headphones in, would be the most enjoyable way to spend both Saturday and Sunday. As we declare the weekend is officially here, I google to find out that 'W' denotes Tungsten and I wonder how I have achieved the four decades of my life without this knowledge but, then again, I have no idea what a fronted adverbial is either and that has served me just as well.

All work and no play – Tabitha Peters, aged 12

21 May, 2020 – The Midas Touch and Rotting Fish

New Zealand has reported five new recoveries, bringing the total number to 1,452. There are 30 active cases with one remaining in hospital. The total number of probable and confirmed cases stands at 1,502 while the death toll remains at 21. (16 May, 2020).

The NHS Confederation warns that time is running out to finalise a test, track and trace strategy to avoid a possible second surge in coronavirus cases.

Following an agreement between the Government and the Swiss pharmaceutical company Roche, a COVID-19 antibody test is made available through the NHS, with health and care staff to be the first to receive it. The test checks to see if someone has had the virus.

The UK stages its ninth weekly Clap for Our Carers event at 8pm.

(Wikipedia, 2020)

The Against All Odds Girl is on King Midas and the Golden Touch. In this Greek blockbuster, King Midas is granted a favour in return for helping the ill and malnourished satyr, which is half-man and half-goat. Midas wishes that everything he touches turns to gold; he has probably been hanging out with Rishi Sunak too much. I consider, however, that he may not be wishing for a pony like the Against All Odds Girl does at every birthday, only to be disappointed, because it is an oddity to spend all of your time with creatures with furry legs, but whatever floats your boat in lockdown.

She reads the story aloud in between bouts of pausing and stumbling over tricky words not to mention losing her place and refusing to use a good old-fashioned finger to keep track. Apparently, this must be done now with a coloured overlay with a pink hue as fingers are redundant in modern teaching techniques. She repeatedly says 'Minus' instead of 'Midas' which is ironic considering that when we see the word 'minus' in the context of primary school subtraction she claims she knows very little about the process. She has demanded two hot chocolates and a comfort break at this point, which involves some Play-Doh that unusually wasn't so hard it could be hurled at the wall and makes a cup and saucer. I wish it was a glass to pour G&T into because I need one right now, even though it is only 10.30am. She then forgets to go to the loo, which was the request for the break in the first place, but I expect she'll save that as an excuse in about five minutes' time to stop work.

The Middle Child is reading Michael Morpurgo's *Private Peaceful*, while eating two boiled eggs. He looks up from his protein fix and says, 'Midas,' (at least someone can pronounce it). 'I have a skin on Fortnite which turns everything into gold. I'm trying to get to level 140 because then it will be fully gold.' The Teenager, who has headphones on and is doing equations with a bored looking teacher, says, 'Yep my skin is fully gold already.'

He adds, 'See I told you that Fortnite is educational, Mum, because it is based on Greek myths.' 'Well,' I say, 'Epic Games may have weaved in some teaching point, but their spelling leaves a lot to be desired because you don't spell a two-week period like that – it's FORTNIGHT not FORTNITE.' The Teenager rolls his eyes and asks, 'Why do you have to make English so perfect?'

The Middle Child has moved on to science. 'Is copper sulphate reversible?' I have no idea and the Against All Odds Girl is distracting me by rubbing her fingers forwards and backwards across her butterfly sequin top. My pupils are being dazzled with flickering lights, sending me into some kind of trance that is fixating my mind on the Play-Doh cup in front of me, while my brain is working overtime wondering why everything today is about transformation when change is outlawed currently, as we relive a series of Groundhog Days. I ask Alexa because she has become my best homeschooling friend and is clearly the genius that I am not. She declares it is reversible and the Middle Child responds 'yes' into the text box. He also likes Alexa because it means his brain doesn't even have to get the cogwheels started.

The Against All Odds Girl looks at the comments made to the fish fossil exercise in which she must order the sequence of events from the fish dying to being immortalised in stone. She lost interest after the fish sank to the bottom of the water and since there were eight stages to label, I end up completing it because I am out of energy and my eyes are finding it hard to re-focus. The teacher responds with a generic feel good, 'well done', but comments that stages six and seven have been mixed up so could she have another look at it. I'm feeling a bit of a failure at primary school education because my mark for the Middle Child's essay on the feelings between the two brothers in *Private Peaceful* was also miserable and sent back with a comment from the teacher to say that he should stick to the strategy that they had learnt in class: point, evidence and explain (PEE) and not go off on some tangent that is not recognisable. I blame it on an inner fear to PEE publicly, especially at school, it just feels ill-mannered. Yet at the same time I don't remember at any point the Middle Child saying that my attempt at his essay was way offline from what they were doing in class. Although, to be fair, he was face down in a TikTok video while I was sweating over his work when the nod of affirmation came. I have now failed Year 3 science and Year 6 English, although I have a degree – so go figure.

It's 4pm and time for the Against All Odds Girl to join in her weekly modern tap dance lesson with the ray of sunshine that is Miss G – she is the Mary Poppins of Essex with pink hair and the sunniest of dispositions, so that when she asks the girls how the homeschooling is going and the answer should be, 'Absolutely terribly and all we do is argue and not do the work,' the girls reply in a sweet chorus, 'Great.' She is the Midas of teaching and I wonder if I can employ her permanently so that the Against All Odds Girl can look at her in that adoring way that contrasts with the venom that normally accompanies our dalliances with the core subjects.

Bullfinch – Oli Manson, aged 6

29 May, 2020 – It's Half-Term 'Init' and We Are All Wacko

Chancellor Rishi Sunak announces that the Coronavirus Job Retention Scheme will end at the end of October.

(Wikipedia, 2020)

It's half-term but not as we know it because the getaway is from the online learning portal to the holiday home that is in the kitchen.

The Against All Odds Girl decides that she will wear her pyjamas for the duration, which is fine by me because it gives me more time in the day if I don't have to negotiate with her to get changed. As we rarely see anyone bar the neighbours, then who's judging? She is making a den in the second holiday home that is the dining room with plentiful blankets strewn up everywhere and weighed down with books that are not read. The Middle Child is in on the act and manipulates his position as the senior by getting her to run the gauntlet to the snack cupboard. I hear him say, 'Wacko,' because the Husband has insisted on lowering food costs by shopping at low-priced supermarkets that carry no brands and apparently don't pay marketing people either because a Twix now has a doppelganger that has a biscuit base with caramel on top and a new name that signals someone is going to get either very high off this or have the key characteristics required to join the cabinet.

'Wacko, Wacko, Wacko,' he keeps saying and she dutifully goes on the covert mission to collect them. I can't be bothered to get cross that they are stuffing down the ill-named snacks because at least I don't have to deliver a lesson on Greek myths or work out the square root of something.

Sadly, the Teenager's school has decided that to follow through with end of year exams is the right thing to do. They fall the week after half-term, so now I am swapping the ones that love the Wacko to the one that must cram in a year's worth of work into a week. It's a total joy, of course, because he insists I help him, a lot, with this. We start with buying a T-shirt in French, 'Puis-je acheter un T-shirt?' The problem is we have had too many of the Wackos and can't stop laughing at the exaggerated pronunciation of 'acheter'. I also note that we won't be 'achet' anything in our favourite low-cost clothing store that is Primark because they have made the sensible decision not to have an online business – great strategy for Coronatime, I think they may employ the same people as the Wacko lot.

We move on to English and Sherlock Holmes: *The Sign of the Four*. I ask the Teenager if he has read it all. He looks at me and elongates the 'Yessss' long enough for me to know the answer is 'non' and English is getting 'nul points'. I do a quick YouTube search and see that the Teenager can circumnavigate the reading part with a quick summary that lasts seven-and-a-half minutes, delivered by a student who may also not have read the book but who am I to argue? If the book is summarised, even badly, it is job done and we are outta here.

I suggest the beach. I announce it as a great treat, and they all reply that they want to stay at home. 'But,' I say, 'We have been at home for ten weeks, surely you want to go out?' 'No,' they chorus back, while swallowing down the last of the Wackos. I live in fear that we may be morphing into the Waltons with a slight leaning towards obesity brought on by the cheap snacks, so I announce there is no choice, and everyone will go happily and delight in the sand under their toes and their sandwiches. We make the 40-minute trip and pitch up – it is windy. Like really, really, windy so the sand is now in everything and not just the sandals. A family come and pitch up beside us and start constructing a windbreak that touches the back of our chairs. When we go and play ball the windbreak family decide they can take up position in our sandcastle and pick up all our buckets and spades. Mum is now taking a photo of this. She sees me coming and apologises, handing back the bucket and spade but we're not in Waitrose and they are not wiping it down. I figure she had been hanging out with Dominic Cummings too much because the apology is delivered with a snarl.

We go home to re-sanitise. I check my emails. The Middle Child is returning to school after half-term. There is a letter about groups of children and coloured bands. The baseline is that they are expected to move around in a cult within their rainbow appointed groups

– not speaking or spitting at each other. It's like being at a holiday club except you don't get to gorge at the buffet bar or take up your entitlement to a sun lounger. The Middle Child is delighted to be seeing his friends but then I drop the bombshell that there are no school lunches and he must take in a packed lunch. 'What, do I really have to eat ham sandwiches for the rest of my life?' 'No,' I say, 'I can do cheese also.' 'Oh Mum,' he groans. 'Well,' I say, 'I could achet some Wackos.' He smiles in acceptance and I think that being high on the caramel biscuit may help the marching in the coloured groupings feel a little lighter.

Takeaways sound good – Tabitha Peters, aged 12

JUNE, 2020

2 June, 2020 – It's Back to School and It's a Game of *Who Wants To Be A Millionaire?*

Figures from the Office for National Statistics show the number of COVID-19 deaths to be at their lowest since March, with 2,872 death certificates mentioning the condition during the week up to 22 May.

MPs vote to end the practice of voting from home, but some politicians criticise the move for excluding those unable to attend Parliament due to age or health reasons. In response, Jacob Rees-Mogg, the Leader of the House, says he will schedule a motion for the following day that will enable them to question the government but not to vote.

(Wikipedia, 2020)

The alarm has gone off, which is a strange siren for my brain to deal with after 11 weeks of being in Groundhog Day where time is not a commodity of any value. The Middle Child is going to school and must be there at 8.35am. This comes as something of a shock to him and to me and is a cruel role reversal because the Husband, who should be up and on a train at 6.30am, is now basking in the glory of being firmly attached to the bed sheets and I am the one that is up before him. He is loving this.

Yet, it isn't school as we know it. It's a version with many oddities attached. There is no school uniform and he is told to wear his PE kit ad infinitum. There's also no school bag with keyring attached of Golden Gate Bridge or names emblazoned in Caps Lock because Smiggle stationery has also been outlawed and clear freezer bags are in. School lunches are also a 'no-no' and we are on a daily sandwich rotation of ham, cheese and ham again. The water fountains have been capped off, too, because physical contact and mutual touching of surfaces is a punishable crime. In this version of school, shouting across social distanced desks is the new normal, colours are in vogue too – the Middle Child is allocated to the 'yellow' group, which appears to be a gathering of mainly boys who prefer cricket to school work.

We roll up and there is a line of children eyeballing each other at two metre markers – close enough to wave, too far to spit. The teacher stands at the classroom doorway giving virtual hugs and dispensing hand sanitiser into sticky palms that haven't touched pencils in weeks. It's like we are queuing for Santa's grotto, but we get a guy in a HAZMAT suit. Ten minutes into the school day and a child coughs. The dominoes are starting to fall. The cougher is sent home because it's lockdown and we need to 'stay alert' (apparently). The school calls us to tell us. 'Oh,' I say, 'Are the neon yellows being shut down?' Because they told us that if someone has it then we all need to stay home for 14 days. I try to infer some care into my responses because I don't want to appear a heathen and the mother that wants to shove their child out the car door *The Dukes of Hazzard* style while cranking up the music and doing a handbrake turn out of the school gates. 'No', the school say, 'They are being tested.' The relief is palpable. I consider WhatsApping the neon yellow parents and telling them we should make a pact to tell our darlings only to cough in the loo or behind a hedge because we need school to be open for our own mental wellbeing and because we are now in a version of *Who Wants To Be A Millionaire?* where if you cough in this 'back to school' version you are out and you don't get to buy a luxury yacht with the proceeds.

School pick-up is a game of Connect 4: white spots have been painted on the grass at social distanced spaces and we must stand on them to collect our darlings, while hoping that someone doesn't block our exit. We can see our parent friends and gesticulate about the tiresome homeschooling, but we need to turn our hearing aids up because everyone hasn't seen each other for months and the chatter is off the scale. Now there is the distance thing too and the white pimples on the grass to deal with, so we are all shouting and white spots are invading our pupils. It's like being at a free rave. The Middle Child appears, less one of his friends who is in jail with Charles Ingram. He announces he has had a great day moving around with the 'yellow' gang. They got to play in the cricket nets, but they can't throw a ball to each other and catch it because that is touching and therefore sharing equipment, which is a big no in Coronaland. This makes sport very tricky although it might not be a bad thing because the skin on their palms is so sore from the frequent school handwashing and hand gel that they can only just about pick up one of the sanitised HB pencils without getting a searing pain.

While the Middle Child has been playing *Who Wants To Be A Millionaire?* and marching with the 'yellow' gang, the Teenager has begun Year 8 exams. This is a game of trust. We trust him that it is not an open book exercise and remind him that he is only 'cheating' himself, although in my head I am thinking that I would like to see a sweep of 80 per cent. It's non-calculator maths, he is using equations to work out the area of part of a trapezium. I 'pop in' to see how he is doing. He points to the question and I have no idea, I sadly can't even do it if I google it. He flicks his hands in disgust that I don't know anything about polygons or maths calculations to assess their area. I feel I wouldn't be much use to Charles Ingram either.

Next up is DT – this is paper-based because design and technology is nothing to do with making anything these days. He has a six-marker resting on the differences between brazing and welding. Once again, I have no idea what either is and wonder if there is an option to phone a friend or ask the audience. Although the audience at home is useless so maybe a 50/50 would be better. At least I can help with geography; the question asks to name three characteristics of a slum. This I can do because as well as the Charles Ingram episode I have watched *Slumdog Millionaire* and the homestead with the chickens and the three children has lapsed into low standards of hygiene, so I tip him the wink – 'Like here,' I say. He nods in agreement and dutifully writes down, 'Low levels of sanitation.'

Grey Squirrel – Oli Manson, aged 6

5 June, 2020 – Perimeters and Corona Books

The number of recorded deaths in the United Kingdom passes 40,000 after rising by 357 to 40,261.

The British Medical Association urges the UK government to extend the rules regarding the wearing of face covering to all situations where social distancing is not possible.

(Wikipedia, 2020)

The Against All Odds Girl is measuring perimeters; 'we', well mainly 'I', measure the sides in centimetres of some rectangles. I ask her to add up the measurements to calculate it correctly. She pauses, flicks her hair, and says she is working it out and adds, 'My life is flashing before my eyes.' I repeat the question, 'What is the perimeter of the shape?' I add the learning tip, 'Add up the sides.' She glances down at the paper, which is a bonus because so far, we have looked everywhere bar the maths sheet. 'What's 22 plus 14?' She laughs, 'I don't know.' I feel I need to bring in the learning support, 'What's 20 plus 10?' 'Well that's easy, it's 30.' I feel the oxygen return to my body. 'Yes,' I say, 'But that's not the whole question.' She takes another intake of breath and tweaks her hair, 'Can I ask Alexa?' I feel the oxygen leaving my body for the second time and say, 'I feel like my life is flashing before my eyes.' And because patience is drying up in Coronaland, I say 'yes,' because the only perimeter I feel that may be useful to know at this point is the biggest ring-fence I can barricade myself into so the kids can't reach me for a while.

Next up is the Teenager's Latin exam, which appears to be something thought up by a pet activist who wants to attend a girls' night out.

Question 12 – translate the following:
a. The women were speaking
b. The god shouts
c. The dog caught sight of the girls
d. The friends were drinking wine
I pride myself in knowing the word for wine in every language (even dead ones) because it is in my opinion a high frequency word that has crucial consequences to the outcome of one's evening and it should therefore be learnt by rote. I tell the Teenager that the answer to d. is 'Et amicos ejus comederent et biberent vinum.' I have no idea about the others or why indeed the god would be shouting or the dog watching the girls. Perhaps the girls were quaffing too much of the vinum and the god and the dog got angry that they weren't included in this merry throng of tipsy ladies.

The Against All Odds Girl moves on to art in which she is required to design a gadget for a pet. She immediately wants to focus her attentions upon the chickens who have become slightly addictive of late, like the vinum. She draws the chicken coop and a mechanical arm and labels it 'egg collector'. I have no idea how the chickens would feel about their perfect eggs being collected with an *Edward Scissorhands* device but since they have been 'free ranging' a lot and taking on everything from the trampoline to the swing, perhaps they will let this one slide.

The end of the week is marked with the class Zoom chat. I pop in to see how the Against All Odds Girl is doing and they all appear to have cushions on their head. I assume the teacher has now run out of quiz questions and this is the next best thing. It is week 11 of lockdown, after all, and we would all be forgiven for the downward slide of education at this point.

Meanwhile, the Husband, who mainly lives upstairs, has given himself a lockdown haircut because nothing can be worse than the one that I did for him in which one side had a wider perimeter then the other. (Do you like what I did there?) This version is far more 'matchy, matchy' and he delights in another self-win. I am pleased because my epic failure at hairdressing means that he will never ask me again. I make a note that the success of marriage is down to boundaries of acceptance and therefore shouldn't the teacher be expressing the significance of this when explaining perimeters to the darlings and referring to the importance of everyone being happy in their own patch, rather than anything to do with numbers?

It's almost time to remove the cushions from the Against All Odds Girl's head and go to the school to pick up the Middle Child, who was dropped off with his luminous yellow band at early o'clock after an emergency phone call to his friend to bring in a book for him as he had forgotten to bring his - the library is permanently closed for fear of cross-corona contamination on the covers of *Harry Potter* books or Roald Dahl novels. We reach the car park and he seems reluctant to join the social distanced queue for the morning rituals of dispensed hand gel. 'What's the matter?' I ask. He says, 'They'll be cross with me if I borrow a book from a friend because they'll know that he has touched it and then also so have I.' 'OK,' I say, 'There are boundaries you have to adhere to, but I think this will be acceptable.' And I wonder how it is that school has become the centre of 'no touching' or 'spitting' that it has, and books are now an item to be mistrusted rather than devoured. Right, must go, chickens to feed and books to jet wash.

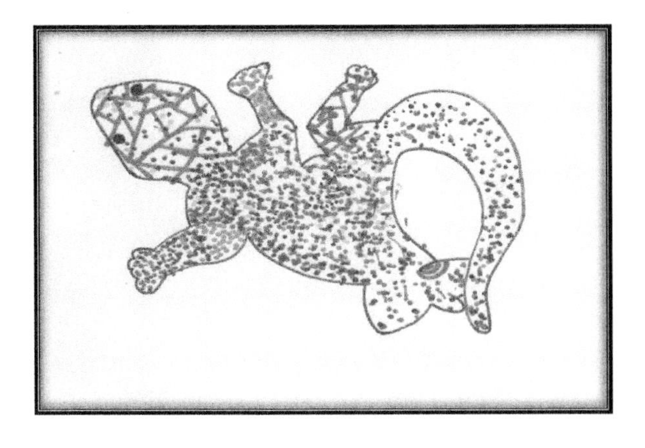

Drawing away the blues – the Against All Odds Girl, aged 8

10 June, 2020 – Sockless Teenagers and Noah's Ark

Professor Neil Ferguson, the government scientist whose advice was crucial in persuading the government to implement the lockdown measures, says that half of the lives lost to COVID-19 could have been saved if the measures had been introduced a week earlier.

(Wikipedia, 2020)

We have reached rock-bottom at the homestead. It's raining and there's not even a Noah's Ark on the horizon to brighten things up – although zoos are open soon, so maybe the animals will pile in and set sail for somewhere more stimulating than Coronaland or being gazed at by social-distancing people who have been locked up for months. I wouldn't blame them. The Teenager hasn't worn a pair of socks for 12 weeks and this is not only because pairs are lacking here but is due to a downward slide into 'slob' status. I am not helping this because I have got to the point when no sock wearing means less washing. The food is also an issue because everyone seems to be in a permanent state of hunger, whether growing or not – I am tired of policing the fridge-foraging and have just let them scavenge like hyenas, until there is nothing left.

Today was a new low point when I nodded an affirmation of the sausage roll that the Teenager was stuffing in between meals and asked if he wanted to join me watching *Loose Women*. He was almost tempted until Ruth Langsford started a discussion on why the panel could no longer share makeup. I thought it was quite interesting and perhaps some light relief from the discussions on whether opening amusement parks and zoos is the right thing to prioritise over children's education. And in answer to this I would say why can't we have an open-air school at the zoo or throw in some maths equations while on Nemesis at Alton Towers and keep everyone happy? Also, perhaps there could be an educational hub within the changing rooms at Primark, to keep the little minds active. Multi-tasking, 'init'.

Lethargy is an issue. The Against All Odds Girl has been slightly rescued from a slip into permanent slobbishness by the introduction of a rotational Maths/English Zoom lesson. This is good for two reasons: she can't argue about wearing her pyjamas all day because there is a visibility issue; and it means that we don't have to endure the daily screaming match when I attempt to teach her. We have returned to the amphibians today and subtraction by 'frog jumping' but now the teaching point is to move away from those with webbed legs and attempt some minusing without jumping over lily pads. She is asked to sort out sums into 'frog' or 'not frog'.

We are doing this while playing *Times Like These* in the background, just to set the mood of melancholy perfectly and get it into perspective that I am spending a Wednesday morning weighing up whether maths is about tailless slimy creatures or anything to do with the bedrock of the economy. Dua Lipa sings, 'I'm a one-way motorway,' and I feel she must be looking in on the maths sheet because every sum is in the 'frog' column and the Against All Odds Girl refuses to entertain the fact that subtraction can be done as a mental exercise of segmenting tens and units and minusing them. The class is asked to come up with different terms for subtraction. One of the girls chips in, 'Compound subtraction.' The silence on the Zoom chat is palpable and the teacher brings the chat back into the realms of 'average' by saying, 'Take away is another term. I like to have one of those every Friday night.'

In English she reads some character descriptions of Mario, Luigi and Bowser and looks up unknown words in a dictionary classifying them as verbs, nouns or adjectives. I offer my *Griffin Savers Oxford Dictionary*, which has a publishing stamp saying 1984. She scoffs at the very idea and says, 'Don't be silly, Mum. We are supposed to use an online dictionary,' because real books with pages are outlawed in modern teaching methods and particularly at a time when libraries are closed. We look up 'lure' and 'fangs' – I wonder if we have slipped into Halloween and I don't know about it because quite frankly it could also be Christmas at this stage, so who knows? The calendar now has everything crossed out with no date against 'term time' or 'school holidays' - it's just one big slobfest day after the next.

We should be attempting one of the many other activities that have been set but the rain refuses to let the general feeling of apathy go, so I suggest a film. She chooses *Frozen II* and I put it on, but they start speaking in Spanish and the Husband is on one of his many calls, maybe to Noah's Ark to see if we can get a cruise in for the summer holidays. We continue to watch it in Spanish because it is beyond my cerebral powers to work out how to turn on the English voiceover. I wonder if she will kick up a fuss because she continues to stare at the screen and doesn't really complain and the Teenager, who I have called upon for help, can't work it out either and his feet look like they are turning blue because he still continues the hatred of sock-wearing despite the downturn in the weather. I knock on the Husband's door and gesticulate to him that the film is in another language and can he help? He looks super-stressed because I am not speaking but I am waving my hands while hand-gesturing a remote control. I think he thinks I am asking him if we can do some Xbox gaming because to be honest this is the desperation of the entertainment levels that we have reached and I am considering joining the Teenager and his sockless friends in a Fortnite marathon, just to tick off some more of the Coronatime.

It's almost time to collect the Middle Child from school. I am thinking at this point that with all the U-turns on whether schools will open or close, like ever, that perhaps I am lucky to have one third of my children in formal education. At least they must wear socks there and you don't have to work out how to explain what the word 'lure' means without it descending into a description of Crimewatch. I leave the Against All Odds Girl staring wide-eyed at the Spanish version of *Frozen*

II and I reflect that this is the closest I am going to get to a holiday abroad this year – still, if there is any sense in the world, the Nightingale hospitals may open as summer schools and the Husband and I can take that ticket on Noah's Ark and set sail for anywhere that isn't Coronaslobland.

Purple Emperor Butterfly – Oli Manson, aged 6

12 June, 2020 – The Repair Shop and Cashless Supermarkets

Figures released by the Office for National Statistics show that the UK economy shrunk by 20.4% in April, the largest monthly contraction on record.

Further ONS figures indicate deprived areas have been hit twice as hard by the COVID-19 epidemic when compared to more affluent areas. The impact has also been greater in urban areas compared to rural areas, with London experiencing the highest number of deaths per 100,000.

(Wikipedia, 2020)

Yet another low today as I find I have put some clementine peel on a 40-degree wash. It has come out quite shiny. I am surprised it wasn't a Quavers crisp packet or a Kit Kat wrapper which have been standard lockdown snacks. This must mean that at least one of my children has had something healthy to eat in 12 weeks, even if it has now been boil washed.

Lush is offering me an online party in place of the actual face-to-face party I had booked for the Against All Odds Girl's birthday. I have no idea how making bath bombs via a Zoom chat will work with eight squealing girls so I think we may have to give that a miss and now I have an expensive voucher to spend in its place – maybe I can buy the bath bombs, deconstruct them and the girls can put them back together at a social distance in the garden. It's a thought and probably better to leave it at that. There's no way they will offer me hardcore cash as it is something to be feared. When I request cashback at Sainsbury's, while buying the Middle Child some packaged yoghurts and cheese for his yellow pod lunch, the till operator (I'm PC with my language) declines my request because that would mean touching something and my fingerprints may be contaminated. Although, this doesn't seem to apply when I can't get the loyalty card to scan, probably because the Perspex screen has put too much distance between my incline on the card and the scanner, and so she offers to assist and whips it out of my hand before I can say 'Coronavirus'. So, go figure, plastic cards are OK to be handled by different human hands but anything that is paper based is a big no-no.

It's Friday, which is fun day for the Against All Odds Girl. That means maths and English consist of crosswords and online maths games, which basically implies the teacher has had enough and is out cycling. I log into the Zoom at 10.30am and am greeted by white noise. I re-check the information and find that the online lesson is only offered Monday to Thursday because school is very much a four-day a week occurrence, which only happens until lunchtime or sometimes until the first hot chocolate is requested.

The Teenager appears to be waking up as half-man, half-boy with some cracks in the voice happening. Most mornings I wonder if we have an intruder asking for jam toast. It's a big week too (if anything can be classed as oversized in lockdown). He is getting his marks back for his online exams. He appears to have nailed calculator maths with 90 per cent and is moving up two maths groups – funny how he appears to have accrued his first 'Outstanding' of the year when it mattered the most. To balance things out he has bombed Latin, so it all looks bona fide. Perhaps the voice was breaking at the point he had to commit 'amo, amas, amat' to some kind of meaning or maybe he was stuffing in the clementine when he should have been doing the dead language comprehension. Either way, the teacher has bought it, so he gets to climb to top set maths and drop Latin for Year 9. He delights in this double win with a yelp that is also 'half man, half boy' so it sounds like a werewolf being partially strangled.

The Against All Odds Girl is drying the chickens with an old dog towel. We no longer have the dog, but the towel remains, and it has been raining. The chickens look a little frazzled at the blow dry but go with it and at least the chicken grooming eats up some of the corona, homeschooling time and she is not asking to construct a diary out of wood, which is the latest creative idea. The Husband has drilled some holes in two bits of old timber upon request and the Against All Odds Girl, who has been watching *The Repair Shop* because even she is bored of repeat episodes of *The Next Step* and has given up channelling a look as a high-kicking Canadian teenager, is planning to thread some string into them and wedge in some of the outlawed 'no-touch' paper and label it as a diary. I don't really know why she wants to do this or why we are entertaining her with the affirmation to go ahead with it, but we do. She continues to thread the string through the holes and hole punch some paper and then sticks 'diary' on the front. She demands £5 for it but I have no cash because Sainsbury's only deal with plastic and I still owe her £s for the perfume made from rosemary, tepid water and dying rose petals. She says, 'That makes £15,' and I say 'OK,' because I am still pulling off the clementine peel from the washed clothes and I can't be bothered to argue.

The Middle Child is delighting in the stories from school when it's sooooo funny that they pulled out a chair before one of the yellow gang could sit on it and he fell on the floor or that they managed to play basketball in the gym and they touched the ball. It's the little things, 'init'. He has requested some more packaged snacks in his lunchbox because he says he has eaten half of them by first break and everyone else has double, hence the trip to the supermarket that is cashless. I cart him off to school with lots of plastic wrappers that say 'mini' on them but wrap his sandwich in a beeswax wrap because I am trying to be environmentally friendly and so now his lunchbox has a ham sandwich with a flowery covering and everything else is packeted except the clementine, which will be going in the washing machine later. It looks like he is off to a Cath Kidston party and then following on to grunge it out at Laser Quest.

Hoping for good news – Tabitha Peters, aged 12

16 June, 2020 – Meringue Bribery and Wimbledon Championships

The low-dose steroid treatment dexamethasone, which has been part of clinical trials for existing drugs that could be used to treat patients with COVID-19, is heralded as a major breakthrough after it was found to cut the number of deaths. Experts estimate up to 5,000 lives may have been saved in the UK had the treatment been used from the outset. Prime Minister Boris Johnson describes the news as a genuine case to celebrate 'a remarkable British scientific achievement'. Dexamethasone will be made available through the NHS, which has a stockpile of 200,000 doses.

Office for National Statistics figures suggest more than 600,000 people have lost their jobs between March and May because of the impact of the COVID-19 outbreak.

(Wikipedia, 2020)

It's 9.26am and the Against All Odds Girl is eating her second meringue of the day. I know this is bad and not in any of the 'good parenting' books but there is also nowhere in the manual that talks about how to cope with eight-year-old girls that have been at home for 12 weeks and need to do column addition. The two are directly linked.

The teacher has decided that as well as introducing frogs for subtraction we now need to partition sums into hundreds, tens and units. What was quite straight forward as 46 plus 23 is now 40 + 20 + 6 + 3 so the sum has a lot of digits and elements and the Against All Odds Girl doesn't know whether to call up the frogs from the pond or peel back every number to its bare bones. It's as though she has mastered riding a bike but then we have put the stabilisers back on and she decides she can't freewheel, after all. This is the point when the sugar is needed.

Breakfast was bread, butter and Nutella, the second breakfast was a pain au chocolat (the closest we have got to French learning) and now we are on meringues. Strands of hair are being coated with Mary Berry delights as she wields her HB pencil to take on the sums. She says, 'Meringues aren't just for pudding,' and I have no response. She then says, 'I'm not doing this method, I'll just do it the normal way.' She does and it's correct but then asks if I can fake the sums using the new teaching method so that she can upload that version because she 'doesn't want to get in trouble'. So I am now doing as I have been told, while hoovering up meringue crumbs from the kitchen chair cushions, and she is on the trampoline because I am no longer in charge of when pudding takes place or how to do maths in 2020.

There's some more soil work to do, too, in which the science teacher, who is now a YouTube sensation, has delivered a 27 minutes and 18 seconds blockbuster about permeability. In the side bar, the popular video sharing platform is feeding the Against All Odds Girl a film on how to make a daisy portrait. This has 274k views, whereas the soil vid is on 23 views, two thumbs up and a thumbs down. She keeps looking adoringly at the video that promises the joy of creating a flowering masterpiece and compares that 274,000 people also thought so, as opposed to the 23 that like the clay, loam and sandy soil premiere. Even I, who have massively lowered parental standards (to be fair they were close to rock bottom pre-coronavirus but at least I can pretend otherwise and put it against 'stress of 24/7 lockdown parenting') doesn't think I can persuade her to do the soil work with yet another sugar hit but we are saved by the bell. I have remembered that there is a class Zoom lesson at 10.30am and so we need to leave the measuring cylinders stuffed with cotton wool and different sized soil particles, as well as the teacher in a gingham shirt.

We tune in to online English. The class is looking at the characters in *The Sword in the Stone* and the teacher is asking the children to describe them by writing a few sentences. The Against All Odds Girl is scowling at me across the laptop and gesticulating writing. I know this means, 'Can you do it?' I shake my head, because I fear the teacher will expose me as a pushover and I also don't want to sit on the kitchen chair with the meringue still on it because I have clean trousers on and that is a rarity in lockdown land. The teacher asks her to 'unmute' herself and asks, 'Are you OK?' She does a thumbs up and I nearly fall over because this is a case of Jekyll and Hyde. She is channelling the venomous personality towards me, while wiping away the meringue from the corners of her mouth and being angelic with the teacher and waxing lyrical about the many attributes of a guy with a beard the length of which would give Rapunzel's long locks a run for their money and a cloak that may have some inside pockets that can store freshly-cooked meringues.

The Teenager is having a saxophone lesson. As the Against All Odds Girl does the thumbs up to the English class, he is performing *Over the Rainbow* to a man with a moustache whom I have never met but comes to our house at midday every Tuesday and looks around our sitting room. I am hoping that the Against All Odds Girl's teacher therefore thinks that we are all under control and harmonious, like the sax tune, with character adjectives flying out of our fingertips rather than the 'muted' reality of meringue-eating hyenas that have only written two sentences, mostly containing the words 'old' and 'magician'. The last of which isn't spelt correctly.

The neighbour's daughter should be in Ibiza pumping out the tunes with her 18-year-old pals as a goodbye to school rite of passage, but instead she has been assigned to teaching the Against All Odds Girl tennis for the afternoon. I am sure she is delighted. I would pay double just for the hour's peace and I need to vacuum up the Mary Berry remnants once more because the ants have started to appear, as has a chicken, which has now entered the homestead, as well as the sax teacher. The tennis coach whips off the Against All Odds Girl and a few of her pals, who can be fitted social distance style within a tennis court. They trot off behind her like she is a female Pied Piper – the Against All Odds Girl does an introduction first and they beam up at the teenage tennis teacher, in direct contrast to the scowling that has accompanied the segmented addition and the character descriptions. I am wondering what her secret is and whether she has any meringues on her, in case there is a downturn at 'Wimbledon', which is happening Centre Court, 2pm.

Cuckoo – Oli Manson, aged 6

19 June, 2020 – Puppy Pressure and Tight Lines

The UK's COVID-19 Alert Level is lowered from Level 4 (severe risk, high transmission) to Level 3 (substantial risk, general circulation), following the agreement of all four Chief Medical Officers. Health Secretary Matt Hancock describes the change as 'a big moment for the country'.

(Wikipedia, 2020)

I'm having a major relationship with someone I have never met and is stored in my phone as 'Joanne Dog'. She is a puppy breeder and is joining my other contacts that are similarly saved according to what they can provide, 'Ian Plumber' and 'John Electrician' are on my frequently contacted list. I am always a little wary of anyone that doesn't have a WhatsApp profile pic and I am beginning to wonder if 'Joanne Dog' is a 70-year-old obese carpenter from Slovenia. Our message exchanges mainly comprise two words per sentence, 'boy, girl?' 'chocolate, brown?' I am winging this, as with many other aspects of my life, and have obviously gone for the cheapest puppy I can buy that doesn't involve taking out a mortgage but am wondering that if I transfer money to the faceless 'Joanne Dog' will I get the 'chocolate' pup in exchange or a wardrobe made from MDF?

The puppy purchase is a direct result of peer pressure and the Against All Odds Girl has been slipping various notes under numerous doors saying, 'puppy'. Just that. She has also got out dog blankets and been searching the internet daily. She is excited when she finds several for £75 but I explain that is a reward for finding stolen dogs. The obsession with pets is easy to see when you earwig into the Against All Odds Girl's Zoom lessons. After a brief daily dalliance with additions, the teacher asks one of the brainy kids to read a million-digit number: '£5,686,342'. 'That would buy a lot of horse boxes,' say not one but several of the children. 'Hacking' is a term they are all familiar with, as is 'pony club'. The teacher chirrups back, 'I like horses, I go to the Hungry Horse most Saturdays.' The enthralled kids roll around laughing but he is having the last laugh on that one.

One of the other children has had to leave the stimulus of the maths lesson to attend to her new sausage dog and so the FaceTiming of pets continues and the Against All Odds Girl looks dewy-eyed and tells me she is the only girl in her class not to have a dog or a horse. I say, 'Don't be silly, of course you're not,' and then I realise that she is and most of them have more than one dog and a horse as well because we are at a rural country school and pets are the replacement for bottles of White Lightning round here. A good job too.

The Middle Child, who is the only person to leave the homestead daily on account of his royal status as a child worthy of being educated (Year 6) has come home with a left shin full of scratches. He says he has had the best day because they played 'manhunt' with the PE teacher, who provides a daily dose of optimism with a smiley face and a bright and sunny disposition that must be hard to maintain while dispensing hand gel to socially distanced 11-year olds. He explains that the joyous event occurred in the forest and his friend pushed him in the bushes and it was 'such fun'. I am revelling in this *Swallows and Amazons* moment and glad that the corona hasn't managed to suck away every aspect of childhood. I am hoping he may save me a few quid and come home with a puppy he finds in there while he is hunting down the man with the yellow gang.

I have started making the fateful error of putting a yoghurt in his lunchbox, which means that when I open up the Arsenal lunchbox it's like a science experiment has gone wrong and every remnant of the yellow pod lunch is coated with some vanilla and fruit split pot. The Middle Child doesn't bat an eyelid or apologise, neither does he when it is repeated the next day or the day after that. To be fair he barely mentions the many scratches and I wonder if he has been downing the White Lightning and become hardy to everything. Perhaps the hand gel is bootleg liquor and when the school door is shut the teacher and the kids get stuck in because pets are not allowed at school, so what else is there to do?

The Teenager says he would prefer a cat. He says this because it winds up the Against All Odds Girl and he loves to see her green eyes flicker and the hair start to swish as the venom builds up. We so far have a split vote, three for the dog, one for a cat and the Husband says he doesn't want anything except a cold beer at the end of the day, mentioning too many responsibilities, before turning right and up the stairs for his next phone call of the day. We have the five chickens and the two small fish. Spotty looks to be on her way out and I must keep tapping the fish tank glass to wake her up and to make sure she is still in the land of the fish that swim. I am wondering if the dog could come asap to soften the blow of the fish that is dying because I am not sure I can locate a stripy replacement in time for the Against All Odds Girl not to notice. Although I fully realise that the Husband would be happier if I just bought a few more fish or some of the £11 chickens because that would be cheaper.

I have been editing a book for a German client who is stored in my phone as 'Daniela Book'. Are you getting the pattern here? She is WhatsApping me a lot and signing off the messages 'waving'. I am not sure what this is or who she is waving at. Perhaps it is a literary thing and I feel I must come up with an equally impressive goodbye message. I am remembering my father, who is a keen fisherman, signing off his fishing emails to his friends, 'tight lines'. Oh how my sister and I laughed when we came across that one but now it could come in useful and I wonder if I could apply this as it denotes wordiness so if she says, 'waving' I can respond with the goodbye that suggests I am a publishing genius. 'Joanne Dog' is signing off our messages with a dog emoji; there is a possibility that I will cross wires as well as lines and show the client a picture of a panting four-legged friend and tell the puppy breeder that I wish to reel in the line.

Three walks a day – Tabitha Peters, aged 12

24 June, 2020 – *The Dukes of Hazzard* School Drop-Off

Scientists at Imperial College London begin human trials of a COVID-19 vaccine after tests on animals indicate an effective immune response; 300 volunteers will take part in the programme.

The British Medical Journal publishes an open letter from health leaders in which they call on the government to launch an urgent review to determine whether the UK is prepared for what they describe as the 'real risk' of a second wave of COVID-19.

The UK government publishes new advice for businesses on how to safely reopen their premises on 4 July.

(Wikipedia, 2020)

The school has asked us to do a drive-by *The Dukes of Hazzard* style and chuck out our Year 3 kids without making a stop, speaking or being visual in any kind of parental way. This I can do. My two favourite pieces of communication during the pandemic have been the letter saying our Year 6 children can return and the one from last week inviting back the Against All Odds Girl for a contact day with her year group. Both forms were filled out in three seconds. You must be in it to win it, I reckon.

It's a double delight because not only do you get to do a handbrake turn in the school car park and shove your child out of the window but you also get to maximise your time without them as you are not invited to hang around. I am 100 per cent in favour of this. I believe the teacher of the Against All Odds Girl and her buddies has had enough, hence the invite to come back to the place that is called school. Yesterday in the class Zoom lesson, the teacher was attempting to teach them how to use delightful adjectives to describe places. He asked them to talk about what they see out of the window. I thought nothing could beat the World War Two bunker that is located somewhere in a tree-lined street in north Essex but there was also the grand finale when the Against All Odds Girl's friend took her laptop out to the garden - or rather the paddock - and Zoomed in her new pony. At this point any learning of adjectives is forgotten and the Against All Odds Girl is snarling at me because I have not produced a 14-hand creature or a military fortification to show and tell. When another of the pupils asks the teacher if he would like to see her new sausage dog, for the seventh time, he groans and shuts down the grammar lesson and declares they must go to a building where no pets are allowed.

The homestead today is a delightful contrast. The Teenager and I are luxuriating in the peace and quiet. Just one slight hiccup when his pen explodes as he has been chewing it in a nervous way because it's online drama and they must do a short 'tabletop' monologue of three characters. He has chosen *Life of Pi*. I thought a 'tabletop' was a sale when you flogged off items that you didn't need and wanted to 'upmarket' the experience from a car boot sale, but at secondary school it's also acting, who knew? From memory he hasn't read the book that Santa gave him with the aforementioned title, so he is winging this from the film. It's at the point when he is waxing lyrical about the Bengal tiger and the relationship with the boy that the black ink seeps into his mouth. I am providing kitchen towel to mop this up but I don't want to be seen on camera, so my hand is outstretched and the drama teacher must be going through various scenarios as to what is going on in the sitting room come school room that now has black ink splattered all over it. The police haven't been called, so I guess he is satisfied.

Still, we won't let this ruin our day because at least I am not fighting with the Against All Odds Girl over maths because she is marching with the yellow gang and chatting about how many pets is too many. It feels very quiet – I can hear the Teenager chewing his Kit Kat in slow motion, which is a strange sound because the braces emphasise every chomp. I am trying to work on the book edit of the 'waving' book client, but the Teenager is distracting me as I feel I am now part of the consumption of the chocolate snack as well as the ink clean-up exercise. He is also clicking the pen that is now redundant and his friend is WhatsApping him during drama because you can 'multi-task' with online school, apparently.

The Middle Child is exiting the building soon that is marked 'primary school' and has been asked to record a short video explaining his best memories, highlights and funniest times. We have had to squeeze him into his school blazer for this event and for most of the parents it appears we have filmed our children from the waist up because the school shorts no longer fit, as the children have been stuffing down the snacks in Coronatime and are now too lardy to fit into traditional school uniform. So now I am filming a child that is half schoolboy and half ready-for-bed in pants and pyjamas. He's an 11-year-old Minotaur discussing how it was soooo funny when one of his friends dared him to eat loads of sunflower seeds and he nearly vomited after taking on the challenge. Funny how being sick is the highlight of your school career. We've done six takes because the instructions are to record no longer then 40-60 seconds and so he misses out his favourite teacher comments, 'sucky up' bit, so he'll probably be branded as the child that was ungrateful and has failed to catapult his 'fave' teachers onto the promotion ladder. Still, it's done, and I haven't had to buy new school shorts for the privilege of the blockbuster on stuffing down seeds.

Greenfinch – Oli Manson, aged 6

30 June, 2020 – Bleached Shirt Signing and Thatcher

As Leicester begins at least two weeks of re-tightened lockdown restrictions, a list of other areas where COVID-19 cases are rising is published, though the increases are much smaller than Leicester's.

Prime Minister Boris Johnson sets out a £5bn post-coronavirus recovery plan for the UK that will see home building and improvements to infrastructure, describing it as a 'new deal'.

Figures from the Office for National Statistics have indicated the number of deaths in the week up to 19 June fell below the five year average for the first time since March.

(Wikipedia, 2020)

The Against All Odds Girl is channelling a dress style with a coral pink penguin T-shirt, skirt and clip-on silver hooped earrings. It's Boden meets Primark. The mixture of genres continues as she has also been watching, *Thatcher: A Very British Revolution* with a particular focus on the Falklands War, which is an odd documentary to be obsessed with for an eight-year-old girl but I'm going with it, alongside everything else. The Thatcher war leadership style is being coupled with an, 'Am I bovvered?' attitude, too, which the Against All Odds Girl is hurling at her schoolwork. It's a poisonous coupling alongside the dodgy dress sense and the earrings are swishing, as she says,

'I don't care though,'
'Come on,' I say,
'I don't care though,'
'But,'
'I'm not bovvered,'
'It's just that,'
'Are you hearing me, I don't care,'
'Please,'
'I'm not BOVVERED.'

She is a cross between the longest-serving British prime minister of the 20th Century and a 15-year-old schoolgirl that is flunking school with a bright pink outfit on. The result is venom and belligerence and the quick conclusion of any attempts at quick-fire maths or meaningful English.

Meanwhile the Middle Child is preparing to leave the primary school building. End of term arrangements have been made to mark the term that never began. It's the film that went straight to DVD release.

Thursday is shirt-signing but obviously picking up marker pens and touching each other's £3 multi-pack, supermarket school shirts is a no-no, so the shirts are to be set out on tables that have been bleached and the children need to bring in their own marker pens. The result is that the 'school shirts' will be put through something of a sheep-dipping exercise so the pens that are poised to scribble 'You're the best' or 'Good luck

BFF' will at best run into one another and the Middle Child will be handed back a shirt with some indecipherable scribble on that stinks of hand sanitiser, detergent and surface wipes.

At least they can give each other presents but these need to be put into sealed bags 72 hours before they are distributed, says the school. Haribo packets and school shirts are the new super spreaders of COVID-19 and goodbye messages are no longer literate. To be fair, the children are so dumbed down after the lack of school they have probably forgotten how to spell the key word spellings that the government benchmarks as appropriate attainment levels for kids that stay at home ad infinitum and who watch political documentaries for entertainment because everything on Netflix has been watched several times over.

The Teenager is apparently on school holidays, although it's only 30 June. I wonder if the school has got the dates wrong – or perhaps they decided enough was enough and that they would put the youngsters out to pasture for a few months more, so the children can hardly speak, let alone write, when they return. If they ever do. He should be going on a fortnight's cricket tour but instead he is tutoring the Against All Odds Girl and her hooped earrings with her, 'I'm not bovvered,' detachment from the school curriculum. His other job of the day is to paint an old shed that is basically decaying and is the habitat for breeding the next pandemic virus. The problem is that 13-year-old boys don't realise that if you paint a wall that means you have to try really hard not to get it on your clothes and/or shoes, so now there is a white trail on the grass, which the 'free ranging' chickens are putting their claws into and making a four-toed pattern across the blades with – the chicken coop looks like the council is laying a new road. Still, it's cheap labour.

Tomorrow the Teenager and his mates get to go to the only place in Britain where you don't have to wear a mask - the aquapark. I hope he can get the paint off his feet before this event or I fear the inflatable gig near Clacton-on-Sea could be shut down as a new symptom of COVID-19 - 'white footprints' - is recognised and appears on the government's list. I said it here first: Clacton could be shut down alongside Leicester in a matter of days.

Click happiness – Tabitha Peters, aged 12

JULY, 2020

19 July, 2020 – It's a School Wrap with a *Lord of the Flies* Meets Sports Direct Sale

The United Nations highlighted the plight of hundreds of thousands of seafarers stranded at sea, some for over a year, due to COVID-19 travel restrictions.

(Wikipedia, 2020)

I've had a bit of writer's fatigue of late, brought on by child and lockdown exhaustion. You get the picture. It may have been to do with the fact that the two schools the three darlings attend, declared a few weeks back the end of term, on the term that hadn't started. I have struggled, therefore, to differentiate the holidays to the school weeks that have already been spent at home. I ain't no Mary Poppins and I have run dry of ideas. My only winning card is that I have upped the consumption of rosé because it's the 'holibobs' and the Against All Odds Girl has well and truly put down her pencil for the duration. It is a double-edged sword because at least we are no longer fighting about maths and English, but we are also not learning - after the term in which we didn't learn, either. When I suggest we do some daily reading to keep the skills on ice she laughs in my face and says, 'You always say that, but you never do it.'

The last day of term for the Middle Child is a choker for two reasons: we have to accept that the new Fitbit watch his friends have bought him for his birthday is well and truly lost and not in his desk; and that he has to march off the primary school premises for the last time, like ever. The 'big fish' in the 'little pond' is about to swim downstream to the sea and find he is mere plankton and there are big sharks about. Having been told that there is categorically nothing to mark this day as the 'last' – 'No' leavers' party, 'No' leavers' residential, 'No' leavers' prize-giving, 'No' leavers' end of school party (thanks for the fun brakes, COVID) - we expect the Middle Child and his yellow pod gang to be given an elbow shake and told to exit the building.

At the last moment, however, some of the more organised mummys decide balloons are in order and so instead of head bowed and a one hop into school, he gets to march in, on this his last day, on a red carpet (well green but who cares, it's just a small thing) and under a joyful arch of multi-coloured balloons that haven't popped or been blown away in the wind. The PE teacher is at the end clapping and swinging his legs to 'upbeat' the moment before slapping on the last of the cheap hand gel that is then smeared down the yellow pod uniform. It's a spectacle and I must say a vast improvement on the 'nothingness' of the planned 'big, fat no' that the school has had to offer.

At the end of the school day - that finishes at normal time because to be COVID-compliant you have to make it the least fun as is humanly possible – the children, who have spent half a term being segregated within their coloured bubbles, are let loose on the school lawn and start to remove their trainers (because school shoes no longer fit and can be asymptomatic so best not go there) and throw them up in the air. Children's trainers are the new university mortar boards and, guess what, no one has checked whether they have been put through sheep dip in case they are virus super spreaders. Naughty! The school rule of not being allowed to throw a ball to a friend to catch and touch it is given a big finger up, as they all begin to hurl their shoes at each other and up in the sky. It's *Lord of the Flies* meets a Sports Direct sale and the looters are en masse.

The headmaster looks ever so slightly awks as camera phones record the 'undistancing' trainer fest. The small group of teachers that is allowed to say goodbye, because they are the only ones prepared to hang with the 11-year olds, start to close in and edge the children towards the car park to cut off the trainer rampage. And so it is that the end of the Middle Child's primary school days is marked with one missing Fitbit watch, one right trainer shoe and a permanent stain of cheap hand gel on his PE shorts.

Muggins here decides it's too much and can't bare the Middle Child to hop home with his one shoe and switch the telly on, so invites the 'yellow pod' round for a hot dog and more of the rosé (for me) that helped me reach an informed decision that throwing a party was a great idea. The Husband, who is on a permanent mission to mend everything and enter some DIY award decides that the trampoline, which is literally in half, can be fixed with an axel grinder and some welding skills. I am now faced with breaking the legs of the 'yellow pod' as they bounce with a sausage in their mouth and one trainer on. Still, and again the wine numbs the impending doom, we are £300 better off because we've had a stay of execution on the trampoline. This makes the Husband happy.

The slap in the face from the last term at primary school does, however, continue when the gazebo ends up in the hedge before the party begins because of course the sun can't shine on their last day. Instead, gale force winds take up residence. The DIY Husband isn't amused when I shout up to him that he must ditch his conference call, which is taking place 'turn right and up the stairs', to sort it. Again, more wine required. After the gazebo is rescued and no one has fractured a bone and all the rosé has been quaffed, we declare the party a success.

The Middle Child knows when to call in more playtime - at 10.30pm, when his mother is half-rosé, half-human – but eventually hits the pillow with a 72-hour sealed Haribo packet that the school says is OK to be distributed by the friends because it has been COVID-sealed and sweated for the aforementioned hours. It's a direct contrast to the trainers that are now strewn around a school playing field in north Essex but who I am to question the science?

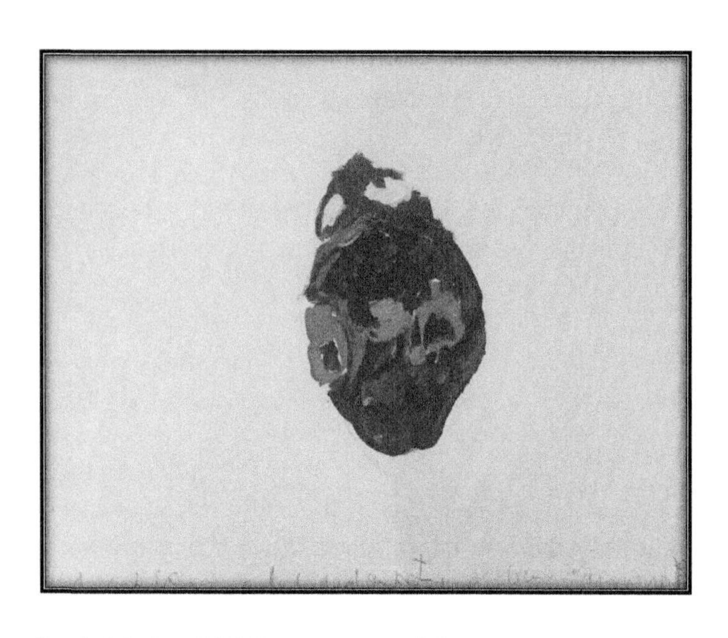

Ladybird – Oli Manson, aged 6

31 July, 2020 – Road Trip Heaven

Alicia Bárcena, head of the UN regional body for Latin America and the Caribbean (ECLAC), while noting that the economic crisis caused by the COVID-19 pandemic was 'pushing millions more into poverty', affirmed that the public health crisis had to be addressed in order to address the economic crisis.

(Wikipedia, 2020)

The Against All Odds Girl has questions about dog castration and the storyline of *Glee*. I 'sent' her on holiday to her aunt's and they binge-watched animal and trash American TV. The boys accompanied her because I wanted to slam-dunk the childcare in one swift move. They learned how to order a Subway sandwich. I feel their education is now complete.

Because I am not good at rocking a COVID-mask suntan line I decided against a holiday to Spain or anywhere else in Europe. The only holiday I felt would be a holiday was if the three darlings went and holidayed without me. It was blissful for me, not for the aunt. I could hear a pin drop and when I tidied their rooms, they stayed like that instead of a tsunami wave of detritus every which way.

I packed a few months' worth of jobs into a few days. We are now reunited, which is clearly a joy, and on our way to the only county in England that is not basking in 33-degree heat: Devon. It has rained en route. I couldn't be bothered to police the, 'what can you buy, what can't you buy,' questions at service stations and beyond so I have dished out the notes that are brown and are handily made of polymer, so they can survive being washed at 60 degrees. The first stop has resulted in the Teenager coming back with four doughnuts, the Middle Child has purchased '3 for 2' packs of Percy Pigs and the Against All Odds Girl a cookie. It's 10.30am and the sugar quotient is high, and we are trapped in a car littered with sugar, pigs' ears and Smarties that have fallen off expensive biscuits. The Husband feels a bit green because he went to the pub the night before with pals and has to mute the radio and the children to receive work calls, while I drive and try to 'cap off' the wild children that are made of E numbers.

We have picked the only day of lockdown when everyone is on a getaway - the four-hour journey is now six and I am in danger of a surfboard hitting me in the back of the neck. I tell the Husband to wind the window back up, which is down because he is desperate for fresh air, and control the children.

'Everyone having fun?' I ask as we enter the county in which it rains constantly. The temperature has dropped by 14 degrees and mist is rolling in. 'Yes,' they say as they stick their heads out the windows, as we navigate the M5 and lick the remaining sugar off the glass.

Summer vibes – Tabitha Peters, aged 12

AUGUST, 2020

24 August, 2020 – Dancing in Caves and Eating Marshmallows

The World Health Organisation announced only a slim possibility of COVID-19 reinfection, citing documented cases of 1 in over 23 million.

(Wikipedia, 2020)

Most people have been on an 'air bridge' to Greece or slipped through the quarantine gaps and made it to France before being sent into lockdown; we bought an American style fridge/freezer and a puppy and spent a week in a cave dodging the rain clouds in Devon. The Husband says enough is enough and it's all about 'choices', so I need to stop moaning. Still the good thing is the fridge is big enough to display my fridge-mounted photos of holidays that we once went on - reminders of happier times, not the photo of us in the cave.

The Husband's key argument to no further holidays is because we have not followed the rules of supply and demand by buying a puppy. The demand is on acid and the price is sky high, so, he says, it's because of our failure to follow the economics that I am not on an air bridge to somewhere where it doesn't rain or there isn't a storm named after a person – I mean I am wondering when it became OK to personify storms and dupe us into the fact that they wouldn't kill off the summer vibes because they had the same name as your next door neighbour.

Still, on the plus side we have a puppy and the Against All Odds Girl is happy. The dog lady who has the faceless WhatsApp profile is real because we had to visit her and the yappers. She rushed out The Kennel Club certificates to bona fide it all, as I sat on the sofa and felt the dog pee seep into my trousers, so that was nice. She keeps sending photos and videos, although to be honest I don't reply because it's too late to ask which one ours is and I am now wondering if she printed off the KC certs from the internet. There is no filter where she is concerned and the vids keep on coming – the one I think is ours, but am not entirely sure, seems to be the one that is the runt of the litter and gets ousted from the pack when it comes to milk time with mum. I am hopeful this is not the case but deep down I think it is her. In short, we have a malnourished pup coming to us that cost as much as a holiday and has some dodgy certificates accompanying her entrance into the world.

On a brighter note, the Teenager says that it is time to go to school. This is a sure sign that the holidays have reached their lowest ebb and we are in a repeat cycle of late breakfast, trampolining, collecting chicken eggs and picking up clothes from the floor. The Against All Odds Girl is filling her time putting on makeup that is at least 20 years old. She has just appeared with a brown tan that she didn't have yesterday. 'Have you put makeup on?' I ask. 'No,' she says, while flicking her green eyes and blending in the last of the 1990s thick, beige foundation into her eyebrows, which are now orange. She also 'likes' Katy Perry and has her *Roar* video on constantly – so it's orange foundation all round while wearing a flower hair band and a grass skirt. The Middle Child is glued to his WhatsApp group for his new school – I am reminding him that in my day you met your new friends on the day you started your school, not before via an online messaging chat but he tells me it's all good. The Middle Child has even made a 'bus friend' without ever having gone on the bus, easing the 'worry' he had been carrying around because the Teenager had announced there was no way he was sitting next to his younger brother on the way to school. Besides, being two years above him, he had earned his right to move two rows back, whereas the Middle Child has to do his time and sit at the front even if that is all alone, which it now isn't.

Our other pastime has been camping in the garden and inhaling melted marshmallows. I was hoping this would make up for the lack of exciting travel but all it has done has sent the Against All Odds Girl into a spin because she is permanently made of E numbers and dancing to *Roar* with her orange tan and marshmallows secreted in her cheeks. I have banned them from hanging out with children who read books because this will make us feel bad and they have been told they can only befriend children who also spend their time eating candy or watching YouTube videos of stunts, including the American gang who have a trampoline in their pool and have to jump from the one in the garden to the one underwater. It's actually quite good.

I am in to name-taping as well as supplying marshmallows, foundation and an internet connection. The new school says it won't sew them on because name tapes are now super spreaders, so I must do it while the wild children dance in the caves and watch stunts being performed or chat to their digital-only pals. The good thing is that while I do this, I can watch the puppy videos, forage in the big fridge and marvel at the water cooler; who knew you needed one?

Dingy Skipper Butterfly – Oli Manson, aged 6

SEPTEMBER, 2020

10 September, 2020 – Back to Skool, Init

Captain Sir Tom Moore carries out his first duty as an honorary colonel, with an inspection of junior soldiers at a graduation ceremony at Harrogate's Army Foundation College.

A paper published by the Scientific Advisory Group for Emergencies suggests Operation Moonshot could lead to 41 per cent of the UK population having to self-isolate needlessly within six months due to the generation of false positives, and warns of potential school closures and workers losing their wages through incorrect test results.

(Wikipedia, 2020)

Sod's law goes like this: the kids go back to school, and BoJo announces a new six-person rule to stop the weary parents getting together. Luckily the Against All Odds Girl and I struggle with maths, so I go for the baker's version when I calculate my half-a-dozen. I'm also into rounding up numbers, so that's all good.

The Against All Odds Girl's teacher emails us before the start of term to ask if we have any anxieties about the return. I promptly reply, 'I'm wondering how loud I can crank up the music when I do my handbrake turn out of the car park and I am ever so slightly worried that the pub won't be open at 8.35am.' I am sure that is the line that most of the parents go for.

The Middle Child has joined the Teenager at big school. The preparations for this momentous occasion began at least four weeks ago. In contrast the Teenager is clearing out the detritus from his rucksack, including a few 2019 Christmas cards (the ill-fated ones that wished us a happy 2020), the eve before school. The compliant Middle Child appears at our bedroom door at around 5.30am fully dressed for the big morning in his shiny new uniform, which is his brother's hand-me-downs with the name crossed out and his put on. The Teenager grunts in his bed when I suggest he gets up an hour after the Middle Child has and tells his brother, 'It will never last.' The tech-savvy school they attend is taking on its own COVID war by declaring pens, pencils and any other Victorian items, including actual paper, banned. We are therefore instructed to buy an expensive digital pen. The Husband, who appears predictably disgusted by the prices that Apple are asking for the boys' pens, rebels and buys a cheaper version because he also makes me shop at supermarkets that are not Waitrose because every penny counts in these COVID-times, he says. Pre-empting the loss of the digital pens, the Husband acquires a pen holder attachment for the iPads. It's like a baby sling for pens. He tests their validity by shaking them up and down several times and declares them 'toddler proof'.

The Middle Child arrives home after the first day, which he declares a stunning success mainly due to the pineapple at lunchtime and the pool table at break time. I peek in his bag because I am his mum and therefore I need to understand his life by examining the contents of his school rucksack. I find the digital pen holder is empty. 'Where is the pen?' I ask. The Middle Child looks up briefly from his new iPad on which the teachers ask if he wants to attend cycling club or the gospel choir. He says, 'In the pen holder.' 'No it's not,' I say, as my heart quickens and I dig around the bag, dodge the fruit winder packet and the clear, wipeable pencil case which is regulation along with the bus face mask and the new maths book with some teacher's name on that I don't recognise. It is now slightly soggy at the corner because the Middle Child, while compliant, is not trained that water bottles, even when empty, always contain a few drops. If you mix that in with your school books something will get wet.

'Come and see,' I say, my face the same colour as the puce fruit winder. 'Oh,' he says, 'I used it on the bus. I was sure I put it back in.' I am deleting the expletives that went off in my head like a hand grenade at that moment. The Husband, who is in his home office, or his 'ivory tower' as the Against All Odds Girl has dubbed it, which she dutifully delivers with a truckload of sarcasm, shouts, 'He hasn't lost it, has he?' 'Yes,' I say, and the Middle Child immediately no longer looks so shiny. The Teenager seizes his moment, glances up from his Instagram and says, 'See, I knew he would slip up.' Cue some crying and inner angst as some 'I-told-you-sos' go back and forth resulting in the Middle Child wailing, while putting his soggy maths book on the radiator.

'Never mind,' I say through many, many gritted teeth. 'These things happen,' (well they don't or only to my children). 'We'll just have to get a new one,' making a note to get the very cheapest on offer because now I know that digital pens are like swimming goggles and gum shields and you can actually pay for a holiday home with the frequent replacements. 'It's a learning curve, isn't it,' I say, tucking up the Middle Child into bed. 'There's just so much to remember,' he says. 'I know,' I say because I read somewhere you must let them learn by mistakes or something like that. I close the door, go downstairs and down two glasses of wine and everything in digital pen land seems better. It's Monday, the only way is up.

Meanwhile, the Against All Odds Girl develops a cold, having not had one for the entire time during lockdown, which is another definition of 'sod's law'. I ask the lovely class teacher, who worries about the returning darlings and their anxiety, if the Against All Odds Girl can stay at school despite the cold or if we have to march to a testing centre because the runny nose is out of control. She explains about temperatures and regulations and in my head, I automatically switch off and think, 'Oh my god, is this seriously happening, just go to school, stay at school, please I have had enough.' At this point I don't actually care if they learn nothing or do anything or lose everything, just go to the building marked school for a few hours so I can have some time to order another expensive piece of kit, buy spot cream for the Teenager and sit in a chair and quietly rock for a few hours. Anyone want to join me?

Can you see my lips move? – Sophie Williams, 12

16 September, 2020 – Primary School Graduation

Appearing before a committee of MPs, Prime Minister Boris Johnson says that a second national lockdown would have 'disastrous' financial consequences for the UK, and that the government is doing 'everything in our power' to avoid that scenario.

(Wikipedia, 2020)

Graduating from primary school in Coronatime involves a wrapped box, a Zoom call and the event happening after you have left. This is a replacement for the face-to-face, celebrity-style applauding that was scheduled for the summer term that didn't occur.

In other years, the 10/11-year-olds who are leaving the primary school building for the last time are made to feel as if they have invented the cure for cancer, while winning the Booker Prize, as they are applauded by a room full of glowing parents and presented with multiple cups and trophies by some Z-list celebrity who has a vague link to the school. Or, if that doesn't work, a retired teacher who can make the allotted time and wax lyrical about how they got beaten with a cane in their day.

Our 2020 COVID version involves a cardboard box that previously contained bottles of wine, the headmaster, a governor, a few teachers who aren't out shopping on that particular Saturday, plus a lady who has rowed the Atlantic for fun, while being sustained on dehydrated meals. I think the link here to the children is that meals are just as grim if you row across the sea as they are in the school canteen.

I send the Middle Child on the school bus, to the new school, with the former wine box that is covered in blue paper and tell him not to lose it like the digital pen. 'OK,' he says and at 10am he dutifully appears in his new school library with some of his transitional primary to senior school pals, who are also carrying huge boxes. It's like Christmas without the turkey, plus barrel loads of social distancing between the children, because in this corona version spacing is paramount when you are opening your pressie. We login from home and the phone rings from the new school as the Husband screen shares on the big TV, so we can imagine we are at the Oscars.

It's the teacher from the new school to say she hasn't got the password to the Zoom despite the many thousands of emails I have sent. It is now the time the Zoom prize-giving should begin, and the Husband is telling me the headmaster is introducing the Atlantic rower who is taking a break from the dehydrated meals. 'It's on an email,' I say to the teacher, who I ask to WhatsApp me that it is all fine because I am a worrier and she is also a friend with a child in the same year as the Teenager so that parent/teacher boundary can be temporarily crossed, particularly when Christmas is in danger of being a flop.

'Got it, we're on,' she messages to me.

The Husband and I, plus the Against All Odds Girl, who is temporarily spinning on her head asking for snacks, settle down to watch the event. After some back-slapping about the term that didn't happen and some further intros to the teachers that aren't buying food in Asda, plus the rower who is still rocking from the 40-foot waves, the prizes are read out. In between each child's accolade, the party of five (they are rehearsing for the rule of six a week early) are clapping. I wince at the awks of this charade because you can hear the sweat grind into the bones when the headteacher claps and then an echo round the empty room. The Middle Child's name is called out, the Husband shouts at me to video it, so now I am videoing the telly while telling the Against All Odds Girl to pipe down about Kit Kats and simultaneously zooming in on the headmaster's hands. If this video gets into the wrong hands it may appear as though I have a hand fetish and an anger management problem.

The Middle Child is awarded the 'Outstanding Prefect' prize – I consider he has got this because he made me buy his class considerable amounts of Haribo to hand out. He also scoops 'Progress in Maths', so I make a mental note to get a maths tutor because he obviously needs to improve and - the grand finale - 'Rugby Player of the Year', which is a silver plate detailing pupils past who also like getting beaten up. The Middle Child, who is an hour away in a school library, tells me later that he was busy spinning the antique plate on one finger because the teachers had left him and his pals unsupervised at this point. The boredom ensued when the prize-giving finished and they wished the headmaster had put on a TikTok video rather than the Atlantic rower because an empty box, some bubble wrap and plateware always wins over life stories when you are almost twelve.

Sadly, after the hero-worshipping that comes with winning the 'Rugby Player of the Year' award came a fall from grace when a few days later the Middle Child loses his second digital pen and tries to frame his brother by stealing his. I have since sent many red-faced emojis to him and discussed that we could consider putting the money into more worthy causes if we continue to buy iPad pens every week of term. A friend messages me to say her son has picked up the Middle Child's shirt at school and I ask if there are two digital pens secreted underneath the collar. 'No,' she says, as I polish his rugby plate and hope that at senior school there is an award for the child that manages never to lose anything because I would happily swap that for the ones he picked up last week.

Peacock Butterfly – Oli Manson, aged 6

24 September, 2020 – Under No Circumstances Must You Cough at School

New regulations come into force, in part, at 5am in England, prohibiting certain 'restricted businesses' and 'restricted services' from carrying on that business or providing that service between the hours of 10pm and 5am. The regulations affect a wide range of establishments, including restaurants, bars, public houses, social clubs, casinos, bingo halls, bowling alleys, cinemas, theatres, concert halls, amusement arcades, funfairs (indoors or outdoors), theme parks and adventure parks. The protected area of Bolton is excluded from the scope of this legislation as additional restrictions apply.

The second version of the NHS contact-tracing app is made available for download by everyone aged 16 or over in England and Wales.

The UK records a further 6,634 cases, the largest daily increase since mass testing began.

(Wikipedia, 2020)

The Against All Odds Girl has recovered from a cold. COVID tests are done by proxy in schools these days. When everyone in the class coughs and has a runny nose, you basically hope that some of the sensible parents will drive their darlings to Aberdeen to have the only available test they can find, at a centre that is miles away from their home and totally inconvenient, because you can't be bothered to drive to Scotland, particularly when Nicola Sturgeon makes it clear she doesn't want you. Luckily everyone in the Against All Odds Girl's class is COVID free, so I no longer must tell her to cough in the loo only or wipe her nose under her desk lid when the teacher's back is turned. She is so used to the silent hack that I think she may have damaged her windpipe from all the inhalation of the croaks. Now she probably has some other respiratory illness that isn't COVID because I have subjected her to the backwards cough for a week.

She has gone from being morose and dramatic about the illness to being livelier than the puppy we are about to collect. I am wondering if we can pass a testing centre on the way to the puppy and do a double-whammy. Now all she wants, apart from a fountain pen that produces green ink, is to have her friends over to play, like every night. Last night she managed to squeeze in two. It's the 'rule of six' – so we are on a rotation. I am not sure whether she really wants the friends to play, or whether it's because she knows that by the time they have gone home I can't be bothered to enforce the spellings and reading on her. It's probably a good thing because on the list this week is 'winch' and 'wrench'. I am wondering if this is the Husband's list for B&Q and we are learning how not to spell DIY words, but I can't ask the teacher because she may ask me about the runny nose, so best not go there.

The Teenager has now called in his runny nose. It's a one in, one out system in this house. A deliberate ploy by them to ensure that the Husband and I are never left alone for longer than a day. Again, I have told him not to visit the health centre or cough in public, under any circumstances. He's been banging on about ethics and how he can easily hook up to Microsoft Teams from home if he is under the weather. 'But,' I say, 'You spent the whole of last term at home and your father and I think it is very important that you go to school.' 'But Mum, it's just the same, I'll still do my work and it's Coronatime and we all have a part to play,' he replies. I am spending my time therefore filtering out internet content that the children may see, to do with staying alert and staying at home. I have also written to his teacher to ask them to stop setting the 'ethics' homework and have taken his temperature morning and night, as has the bus driver, to prove he is OK, as well as given a long explanation about the meaning of the word 'persistent'.

He got a merit this week for a 'great attempt at using causation language in history'. I explain this is great and that I also have some vocabulary for the period in history we are currently living through but I am not sure it would warrant a merit due to the range of expletives that are attached, particularly the vocab that was used at the homestead when we learnt of the 10pm curfew at the pub. Although, like the 'rule of six', we are getting around this with a 6pm kick-off. BoJo has done us a favour as we are all done and dusted by 10pm and ready to climb into bed early doors.

Just to make everything seem better and to have something to look forward to, Christmas is also cancelled because we are a family of five, so we can only issue one golden ticket. I'm thinking that the only way to have both parents this year is to kill the turkey and have a funeral because then we can have up to 30 people. To be honest, after the news that the six months we have done isn't enough and we have to start again, I am ready to slaughter something, anything. If I can't find a turkey then one of our five chickens will do, especially as just as BoJo tells us to hunker down for another innings they decide to stop laying eggs. The whole of my homestead is on protest, while inhaling their coughs in reverse and so I need to follow suit and inhale, too … a vat of wine should do the trick.

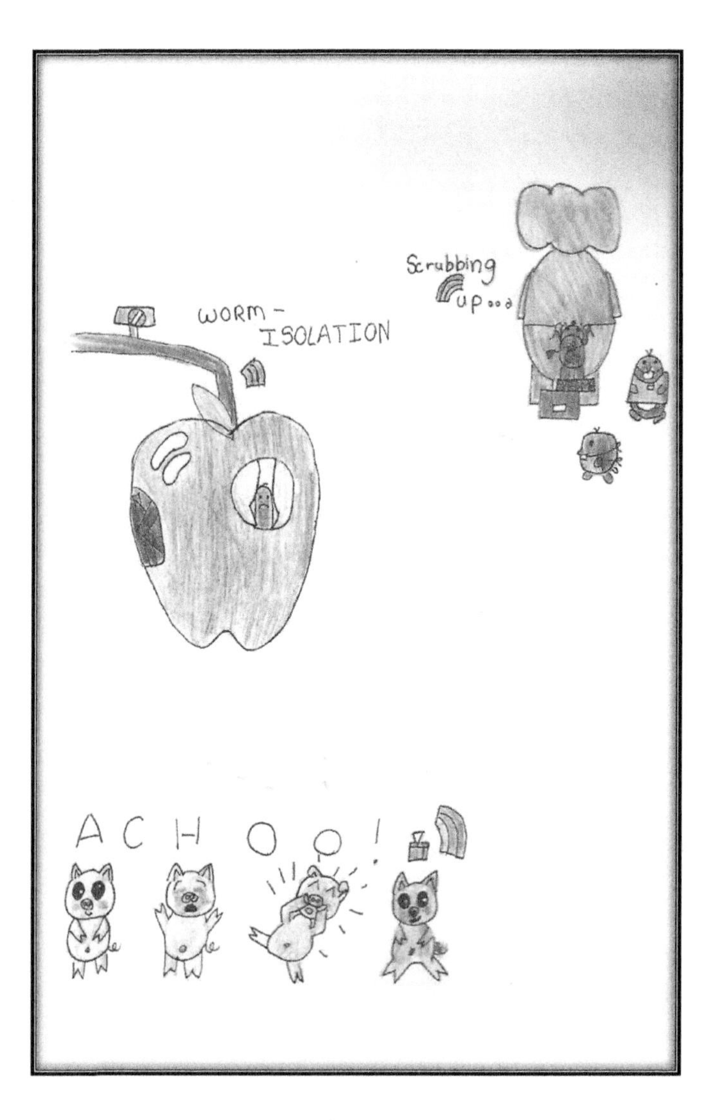

Isolation loneliness – Tabitha Peters, aged 12

OCTOBER, 2020

1 October, 2020 – Puppy Pee and Glastonbury

A study of COVID cases by Imperial College London, the largest of its type in England to date, suggests the spread of the virus may be slowing. The study also suggests the R *number has fallen since measures such as the 'rule of six' were introduced, but warns infections are still high, at an estimated 1 in 200 people.*

Boris Johnson's father, Stanley Johnson, issues an apology after he was pictured in a shop without a face covering, while former Labour Party leader, Jeremy Corbyn, apologises after holding a dinner party attended by more than six people.

Scottish National Party MP, Margaret Ferrier, is suspended from the party after it emerged she travelled by train from her constituency to Westminster while experiencing COVID symptoms; Ferrier says there is 'no excuse' for her behaviour.

Teaching unions have been angered by government plans to use emergency powers under the Coronavirus Act 2020 to force schools to offer online lessons as well as face-to-face teaching; one in six secondary schools are closed to some pupils because of COVID-19.

(Wikipedia, 2020)

As the puppy is christening the limestone, tiled flooring in our kitchen, the Against All Odds Girl is vomiting in the upstairs bathroom. I am running the gauntlet between the two, mopping up dog wee with one hand

and holding back the girl's hair with the other while inwardly retching myself and wondering why I wasn't a stellar lawyer who had people to do this for me. Meanwhile the Husband is watching *Britain's Got Talent* and pouring himself another glass of Malbec. I want to take the bottle and down it in a dark corner of the house, away from humans and animals.

When your child is being sick and the dog that she wanted is weeing, simultaneously, but in different rooms, what you don't want is the two boys that you also have, to start asking if they can have crisps because they want to join the Husband (who isn't helping) watch *Britain's Got Talent* on the comfy sofa. I say, 'Yes,' of course, because I want an easy life and I am fast-forwarding the evening to the bit when I have finished scrubbing out the Against All Odds Girl's pasta vomit from the carpet, have sprayed the kitchen floor with disinfectant and hoovered up bits of smoky bacon Walkers crisps from in between the sofa cushions. This is the order of events before you get to catch the Husband up on the Malbec drinkathon. By this time, you have sick underneath your fingernails and dog wee smell pretty much everywhere and your body odour is now a cross between a gone-off curry and the men's urinals.

Of course, the puppy is all worth it. I mean, all worth it. She is cute, I mean super cute, but she bites, and she wees - you already know this - she then bites, and she then wees again. She is on a Groundhog Day of her own. I am sniffing, excuse the pun, the coming of a second lockdown because in the first we got the five chickens and the Husband ordered in gin and now we have the puppy and a case of red wine has arrived in the post. I make a note to send a memo to Chris Whitty to tell him of my scientific hunch. To be fair, there are so many animals at the homestead now that, coronavirus or no coronavirus we are locked down semi-permanently, so best get on with it and get the loo roll in.

At least the school is open for now. I have signed the Against All Odds Girl up for pretty much every club going to extend her school day, because I now have to allocate more time to mopping up dog wee and quite frankly I want all the children out of the house for as many hours as any place marked school will have them. Yesterday, was ballet. This means that you are legally allowed to cross a school bubble and go to the main building to pick up your dancing queen. It feels naughty. It's the small things, these days. I realise how long it has been since I have stepped foot in these hallowed grounds because the maths teacher has grown his hair quite considerably. I thought he must be someone new or someone that was hoping to find Glastonbury located within the quiet grounds of a north Essex primary school but hadn't got the memo about the cancellation. He waves at me and I wave at him with the fingers that smell of wee and vomit. From a socially distanced meterage, he thankfully doesn't get a waft of the stench.

My eyes squint as I try to work out if it is really him. We have only been in communication via the hapless online maths system. My heart starts to shudder as I begin to remember the dark days of the homeschooling and the daily wrangling about the equations and the column addition. I recall the hours that had gone by when we failed to upload or download the required work and so I think I best not go there, a bit like taking the Against All Odds Girl in with her runny nose to the teacher that cares about their anxiety levels, so I opt for a three-fingered wave and head off to the collection point, except I arrive at the wrong classroom and come across the PE teacher, whom I also haven't seen for six months.

It's defo a bit of a Friends Reunited moment on mute, because in his position as deputy head I can see an internal battle brewing. Half the parents, whom he hasn't seen for six months, are now in the wrong bubble and, with their finger-waving and muddy footsteps, are potentially contaminating the other year groups. He quickly hurries us to the correct place, which is also technically out of bounds but OK on a Wednesday afternoon at 5.10pm, a bit like the 10pm pub curfew except if you are in a Parliament bar, because in these places and at these times COVID doesn't exist and the rules are temporarily halted.

I scoop up the Against All Odds Girl in her character dance skirt and clippy, cloppy shoes. She flicks her hair in delight at the outfit and the rekindled love with the lovely ballet teacher. We then walk the gauntlet of the illegal car park in the rain, to the legal one that is in a field in Suffolk because we are on the border between two counties and therefore you are either in the posh bit or the not so posh bit, depending upon which class you are attending. The rain starts soaking into the shoes and the ribboned skirt and I have been too busy researching dog pee disinfectant spray to pack an umbrella. The maths teacher keeps waving and so now I think we probably are in Glastonbury like he thought, except I have a slightly damp eight-year-old girl with me with her hair in a bun that is starting to slide and a maths teacher that is chasing me for the Middle Child's lockdown work. So, I make a run for it. We eventually find the worst car in the car park, the one with the rust on it and the comedy items that fall out when you open the door, like glue stick lids and stale brioche rolls. We get in it before anyone realises it's not a Range Rover or the maths teacher finds us.

Back home, the puppy greets us with another wee on the floor and a hand bite. The Against All Odds Girl says she feels a bit queasy after the dancing in the skirt and eating the gone-off snack in the sub-standard car. So, I say, 'Why don't you have an early night?' It's not Glastonbury and I can't do the double-whammy vomit and dog wee shift again. My fingers still smell and, quite frankly, I've had enough. There is a case of red wine that is winking at me and, if I down it quickly enough, I'll forget that I smell of animal urine and that the maths teacher wants blood.

Lion’s Mane Jellyfish – Oli Manson, aged 6

7 October, 2020 – Moaning Myrtle and the Puppy NCT Group

A problem with the UK's sole distribution centre for pharmaceutical company Roche, in Sussex, has led to a significant decrease in the capacity to process COVID-19 assays, swabs and reagents, which has meant that Roche have alerted the NHS of the shortage. According to the company, it could be two to three weeks before the supply chain issues are resolved.

Pub retailer, Greene King, announces the loss of 800 jobs, citing the impact of tighter lockdown measures as the reason. The brewer has closed 79 pubs temporarily, a third of which it says will remain shut on a permanent basis.

The UK government announces the establishment of the Global Travel Taskforce to look at introducing a COVID-19 testing system for travellers to the UK, giving them the chance to spend less time in self-isolation if they receive a negative test.

(Wikipedia, 2020)

The Against All Odds Girl believes the school loo is haunted. The friends of the daughter have stirred the rumours that an equivalent of Moaning Myrtle is hiding in the toilet bowl. The lovely class teacher, who gives them the time of day to hear about the ghosts of pupils' past, which may be lurking in the porcelain cistern, has suggested that they go to the washrooms in pairs. The Against All Odds Girl thinks this is great because during the maths lesson, in which she dreams about the unicorn highlighter pens she desires, while the teacher is droning on about the 24-hour clock, she manages to pop off to the loo with her pal, who also prefers stationery to work. She then spends a lot of time pretending to be on a *Ghostbusters* mission, checking behind, underneath and on top of everything, to find that when they have completed their covert mission, the maths lesson has expired and it is now Art and DT, during which, funnily enough, they don't feel the need, in this their favourite lesson, to nip off to check out how loudly Myrtle is moaning.

Meanwhile, the Teenager is studying *Lord of the Flies* and writes a paragraph to describe the way that William Golding shows the boys' fear. He begins with examples of personification, including how the flames 'leap and creep' to humanise the surroundings and evoke fear. I say, 'What about when Roger moves the boulder, deliberately, and drops it on to Piggy? Doesn't that show the fear and evil?' 'No, Mum,' he says, 'You don't get it, you have to be more subtle then that. It's all about the build-up,' because apparently in GCSE English you mustn't address the squashed boy in the room, you have to spend a whole page pretending that bit doesn't happen. I am slightly distracted when I argue this point because the 'cocker puppies' group has accumulated a further 14 WhatsApp messages. It's like an NCT group for dogs, where the new owners ask if it's normal if the puppy chews or whines at night and then each person replies with their own little piece of advice and/or video, if you are lucky.

The Teenager is now going on about how the palm trees are said to be reclining and compares this to people doing the same. I am silencing the puppy group and try to shush the Middle Child who has just appeared and says he needs more food after the dinner of stodge: pork chop and mashed potato because it's autumn and we are layering up the clothes to hide the blubber. 'Make some toast,' I say, as the Teenager adds, 'I thought you said you were good at English.' I bark back, 'Just stick down the bit about them killing each other.' The Against All Odds Girl pipes up, 'Mum that's horrible, that's how ghosts are made, someone is killed before their time and they become a ghost, like the one in our loos at school.'

Bob is showing me a photo of his puppy retrieving a plastic duck. I have no idea who Bob is and wonder how it is that smartphones make it OK to connect with strangers and show them photos of pets eating PVC birds. 'Ghosts aren't real,' I say to quieten the daughter who is a quarter of an hour past her bedtime, which she doesn't understand because she keeps skipping the lessons on clocks, to spy on Myrtle. 'Yes, they are, all my friends say so,' she replies. 'Well they also say that you should buy unicorn highlighters, just like theirs, and you really don't have to,' I quickly respond. 'I do,' she says, 'We are counting the number of times we hear a noise and we highlight it with a different colour each day.'

'Figurative language,' shouts the Teenager, while he simultaneously scrolls Instagram for friends showcasing better evenings. 'Right, put that down,' I say because actual blood clearly doesn't show fear in modern day English. The Middle Child is stuffing in the second supper of toast and tells me that it's so funny that our lift-sharing parent neighbour uses funny voices when he asks his daily question, 'How was your day?' I make a mental note to do the same with the neighbour's daughter at 7am on the morning shift but know that, in reality, I won't be exchanging any pleasantries, because on our homestead we will have been shouting at each other about why everyone is not ready and in the car at the right time, leaving just a hoarse croak like Myrtle's, which won't be useful for impersonating anyone.

The Middle Child wipes his mouth on his sleeve to soak up the butter and delivers the final blow of the day: 'By the way, my pen is broken.' I look up from Bob and his puppy and say, 'Sorry, are you joking?' 'No, I dropped it and it snapped,' he explains. He produces the digital pen and the nib, or whatever the pointy bit is called in digital pen land. This now looks like Myrtle's face after she has been in the u-bend for too long. 'I can't believe this,' I say, as the puppy video is interrupted by a friend who messages me to ask for the brand of cheap pen that we now use, on account of the frequent purchases. I reply with a sad face emoji but secretly do a dance in celebration of the fact that I am not the only one. In my head, I bellow out one of Myrtle's screams that pen-gate rumbles on, like the ghost tales of the daughter's class.

Lockdown puppies – Sophie Williams, aged 12

15 October, 2020 – Nits and the Labour Leader

A study by University College London reveals that up to 17 per cent of the population of the UK could refuse to be immunised by a COVID-19 vaccine.

Italy, Vatican City and San Marino are removed from the quarantine exemption list following a rise in COVID-19 cases in Italy.

The House of Commons announces plans to stop selling alcohol in its bars and restaurants amid tighter COVID restrictions for London.

The Metropolitan Police says it will take no further action against MP Margaret Ferrier for her breach of COVID-19 rules.

(Wikipedia, 2020)

The Against All Odds Girl has a shower cap on and is blowing bubble gum. She has nits. This means she is not at school until the critters that are resident in her scalp depart. I am combing out hair lice while asking her to learn how to spell 'Powerpoint'. She is not listening or spelling the word that she doesn't have any use for but focusing on moulding the gum to the end of her tongue. I am trying not to retch as I persuade the wingless parasites to leave her locks. I am aware half-term is looming, plus another lockdown, and I want to make use of the days when the place called school is still open. Currently it is in some kind of swamp in north Essex because the segregated drop-offs have made the field that we park in like a Tough Mudder assault course.

This means the Against All Odds Girl needs to try and make it to the classroom door without both nits and falling flat on her face in the mud. We are failing to accomplish either. She is lying on the sofa, with a shower cap on designed to suffocate the nits, the bubble gum in her mouth and watching Mary Poppins make dolphins emerge from the bathtub.

'Can I go back to school this afternoon?'
'No.'
'Why not? I want to go to ballet.'
'Because you have nits, and everyone knows.'
'How do they know?'

At this point I can't tell her that I have told the lovely class teacher who worries about their anxiety levels that the Against All Odds Girl is fighting her own battle against the hatching insects and that the whole school now has a letter saying a 'case' has been reported.

'They won't know if we don't tell them.'

'Have some more bubble gum,' I say and wonder if I ought to consider a new school for her to go to, where they don't know she has nits or ever has had the nits.

The Teenager wants two friends over for his birthday in November. I call in a favour to ship off the brother and sister for that night to a family whose eldest son is away at school. They are the family of five who are temporarily four and I am a family of five who needs to shed one. It's a *Jumanji* jigsaw in which you will either get a fine, a swarm of bats or nits – take your pick. The WhatsApp messages start to ping as I consider how to kill off the other children in order to allow the Teenager to rock out on his 14th birthday and the mummy friends start to discuss if Keir Starmer is hot in a middle-aged kinda way (we've already decided BoJo is a 'no no'). I debate this when the Middle Child appears and tells me he needs a new pencil case for the digital pen because the strap on the iPad clearly doesn't work. We are on the fourth of these fine items of stationery and so he needs to re-work his entire pen-carrying system. I say 'OK' while I reply to the mummy group that fancies the Labour leader, 'Well only in this photo' (in which I will grant he looks a bit like David Hasselhoff). The Against All Odds Girl is now spinning on her head in the shower cap and stretching the bubble gum from one armchair (the newly reupholstered one) to the other. The puppy is trying to jump over it but ends up ricocheting off the furniture and licking it. I make a note to get the kids worming tablets, as well as more nit cream and the poster of Keir.

The daughter tells me that she needs new ballet shoes. 'I've ordered them,' I say smugly and then wonder where the heck they are. I look at the Amazon order list and realise they are not arriving until the end of December, after the Teenager's birthday in which we must dispense with the younger two or murder them. I go to the school shop after managing not to fall head over arse in the mud and shout out my order at the cabin door. I am muffled by the mask I am wearing, despite the fact that we are outside, but there is always a risk of COVID when you are ordering pink dancing shoes, which incidentally they haven't got in stock because they are made in Wuhan and we know how that one ended up. 'Lucky that I am missing ballet today, because I haven't got any shoes,' the Against All Odds Girl says with a touch of venom as she scratches her scalp through the plastic of the shower cap. 'Yes, I suppose so,' I reply, wondering how she has turned contracting nits into something to be self-congratulatory about.

Under the weather – Tabitha Peters, aged 12

21 October, 2020 – Wet Children and Chocolate Ganache

Trials of a COVID-19 vaccine being developed by AstraZeneca and Oxford University are to continue following a review into the death of a volunteer in Brazil. Details of the death have not been disclosed, but Oxford University says a 'careful assessment' of the circumstances has revealed no safety concerns.

A further 26,688 COVID-19 cases are recorded, the highest daily figure so far.

(Wikipedia, 2020)

It's 6.31am and I make my weary way across the cold, tiled floor to the utility room, where I am hoping to find the sports kit, that is now the four-day-a-week uniform, dry. It is not. This wakes me up. It is damp, the type of wet which creeps into your bones and sticks to your skeleton. I am wondering if the 'cupboard dry' setting I used should be crossed out and be re-written, 'kinda wet'. I blame the Husband because he likes change, I do not. He suggested the different setting, whereas I, like most people in Britain use the same washing, tumble dryer and oven setting for everything. End of. This is a game changer to the morning routine. I wake the boys up and tell them to do everything in reverse to give more time to the drying, which is now on speed.

I stand by the machine in the hope that by osmosis and my presence it will suck out some of the moisture. I periodically empty the machine and randomly scatter the important items like the PE top and shorts on the radiator, in the hope that a split strategy to wet-gate will work. It doesn't. It's 6.55am. It's still not dry. The boys are banging their pyjama-clad legs against the wall and looking at Instagram of people that have got their s**t together and go to school wearing dry clothes. The Teenager says, 'Mum, I told you not to wash my kit during the week.' 'Well excuse me for trying to ensure you are clean and tidy and this wouldn't have happened if you actually wore school trousers, shirt and jumper like you should do, instead of PE kit every day.' I mean, do we get a refund on the uniform that is now outlawed as a super spreader?

I know that the neighbour's daughter will be waiting (in the rain) to be picked up for the bus in four minutes. I shout up to the Husband that we will have to drive the boys in because they are wearing PJs and their kit is not dry. 'Are you having a laugh?' he asks. 'I am not,' I say as I get into the car to take the child that isn't mine to the bus. The ridiculousness of this doesn't faze me, which is worrying. She's not there; I wonder if it's a conspiracy and she is also drying her clothes, but the truth is she has overslept, like a normal teenager. We arrange that when she is awake and the clothes are dry, we will drive the children to the school.

The Husband is now on high alert. He is mopping up the puppy pee while assessing the status of the slightly damp clothes. 'Oh, it's fine,' he says. I raise my eyebrows because not even I can send the boys to school with clothes that seep water. My phone goes, it's the 'Pasties and other things' WhatsApp group, aka the family group: my parents and sister. It's basically a chat group showcasing food and mentioning birthday presents at the same time. My dad is sending over an image of Michel Roux's au chocolat dessert. I feel like face-planting in it. The Husband says, 'You shouldn't bother washing the clothes midweek.' At this point I throw the car keys across the Silestone kitchen island, which, unlike the clothes, promises not to be porous, and say, 'That's it, you drive them. I've had enough.' I shove the soggy children into the car and he helpfully adds, 'I'll stick the car heater on and they'll dry on the way.' 'Either that or the boys' hair will be sticking up like a loo brush while they die of pneumonia,' I add.

The Against All Odds Girl pitches up at 7.31am. Her clothes are dry. This is good for my mental health. It's the last day of term for her. She is doing a sponsored walk, in the rain. This means that the only child in the house not to be wearing clothes that are wringing wet is about to do just that – and, to ensure consistency, I forget to pack the bag of dry kit to change into, as the school has suggested. She makes a quick trip into the garden and comes back with some twigs; they are also damp. 'What are you doing?' I ask, looking up briefly from the picture of the chocolate sensation. 'I am giving out awards for the 'bug club' at school.' 'What, with sticks?' I say, trying to ignore her stuffing them into a plastic bag with envelopes written out to her girl gang, who apparently all fancy themselves as junior versions of Sir David Attenborough. 'Yes,' she says, 'I'm in charge,' and her head visibly grows a couple of inches. 'Fine,' I say and hurry into the car because her trainers are now damp from the nature forage and I think it's best not to go there with the mother guilt of all my children going to school semi-wet.

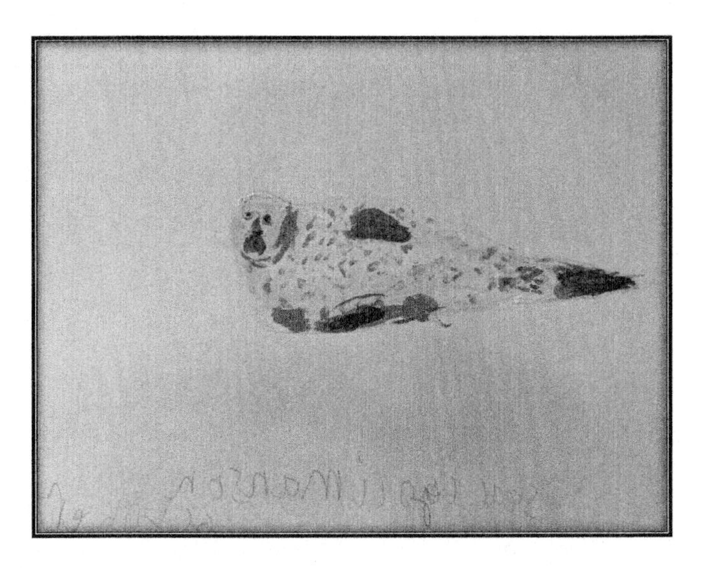

Common Seal – Oli Manson, aged 6

29 October, 2020 - Everyone Having Fun? Half-Term and Wild Seas

A study by Imperial College London suggests there are 100,000 new COVID-19 cases in England each day, with the number of cases doubling every nine days.

An updated version of the NHS COVID-19 contact tracing app will issue more self-isolation notices, its new boss, Gaby Appleton, has said.

Cyprus and Lithuania are removed from the quarantine exemption list, the change taking effect from 4am on Sunday 1 November.

Model railway maker Hornby reports a 33% increase in profits during the six months up to September 2020 as more people take up hobbies during lockdown.

(Wikipedia, 2020)

It's 2.01pm. I am sitting in our car looking at the beach we are supposed to be going to. There is no beach, however, because we haven't looked at the tide timetable and the waves have submerged any glint of sand. I contemplate sitting on the rocks because, you know, we are here, so the show must go on. I put the car into 'P' as the rain hits. The Husband gives me the 'look' - I return it to ensure we are 'matchy matchy' on the expressions of disgust. The children declare they want to go 'in' just as the weather turns into a proper storm - the surfers are out but no children. I say 'OK,' while weighing up the possibility of having to send the coastguard in and getting a telling off, versus the torture of being trapped inside the rust bucket any longer with three children who are eating cherry colas and asking if they can buy an ice cream, in October.

The Against All Odds Girl contorts her entire body to reach into the boot for the bag that contains the wetsuits, in a nod to forceful decision-making. The puppy has been busy pulling out the towels and destroying them and peeks over to look at us, with a bright red, Primark towelling thread visible in the corner of her mouth - I am fully expecting she has also peed on them. The three begin to get changed in the back seat. I say, 'Fold up your clothes and put them in the bag,' as I see the new Joules top with the flicky sequins on it, trodden into the rubber matting of the car floor - a cherry cola stuck to the underside and some grains of Devon sand mixed in. They open the car door and my swimsuit hits the kerb because at this point all dignity has gone.

The children thump their chests in a moment of coolness, '*Point Break*, init.' I am aware, however, they are minus the surfing talent. The Husband asks if I am worried about the free ranging chickens that we have left home alone at the homestead. I roll my eyes at him as I witness the three, human children enter the wild sea and wonder how you get to a point in parenting when you are more concerned about poultry then the children you could go to prison for, because you needed them to do an 'activity' and the trampoline park was too much of a drive away.

It's 2.23pm - the Against All Odds Girl says she is cold. She clambers into the car and begins to strip off the wetsuit, grinding more of the sand into her expensive, new top. She grabs the scarlet item - which the puppy is now bored of - and begins to dry herself with the pee-soaked fluffiness. She sniffs the air as the boys turn up, which is a good thing because they have not been visible all this time. They use my swimsuit, which is still on the kerb, as a floor mat and the car begins to shake as various limbs fight to be dried by urine-covered towels.

We head home and spend the next two-and-a-half hours warming up from an activity that lasted just 25 minutes. I have a look at Facebook for activities to do when you are in a holiday county in which it rains - it feeds me with ideas on how to carve pumpkins into the face of Elvis Presley or fairytale castles. I grab the puppy and use her as an excuse when the Against All Odds Girl catches sight of the pumpkin sensations and suggests we do similar. 'Sorry,' I say, 'No can do, the puppy is asleep on me, I can't move.' 'OK,' she says, 'We'll do it later.' I make a mental note to take them wild swimming again, as soon as she mentions this hideous pumpkin idea for a second time.

All alone – Tabitha Peters, aged 12

NOVEMBER, 2020

10 November, 2020 – Blind Pick-Ups and Sad Face Speeding

Health Secretary, Matt Hancock, announces that the NHS is ready to begin providing the COVID vaccine 'as fast as safely possible'.

Figures from the Office for National Statistics show the number of COVID-related deaths has exceeded 1,000 for the first time since June, with 1,379 deaths in the week ending 30 October, accounting for 12.7% of UK deaths in that week.

Figures show that UK unemployment stood at 4.8% in the three months to September 2020, up from 4.5%, as a result of the COVID crisis.

A group of Conservative MPs who voted against England's second lockdown have formed the COVID Recovery Group, to argue for a different approach to dealing with the virus once restrictions end on 2 December, one that will enable society to 'live with the virus'.

(Wikipedia, 2020)

The school's speedometer hates me. I am wondering if it is faulty because I have never seen it smile. This is not helping raise the COVID mood at 8.25am, like each day. I can't work out how to drive any slowwwwwwwwwwwwer and raise a grin. I am considering leaving the car at the bottom of the hill and walking past the speedometer to see if it is set on the face of doom permanently – but stepping outside the car is also outlawed in this new school drop-off routine.

The Against All Odds Girl is not helping to boost the spirits either because she refuses to buckle up her school bag. We drive by the sad face. She says, 'Mum, you're speeding again.' I say, 'No I'm not. It's not possible to drive at five miles per hour, unless you want another car attached to your rear.' 'What's your rear?' she asks peeking at my sizeable behind. 'It means different things. Not just bottom.' 'Oh,' she says, looking disappointed that a 4x4 won't literally be plastered to my derriere.

We get to the drop-off point, having followed the many arrows that signal if you are COVID friendly or not, on account of whether you can open your car door. I do the daily reach back behind the driver's seat for the school bag; it is empty. I am feeling the urgency of the other cars building up behind us, whose drivers have also been greeted by snarly face speedometers to cement the levels of deep-seated melancholy. The receiving PE teacher wants to get the hand gel into the girl's sweaty palms and count in the next vehicle and gives me the 'please leave' look. I decide the shame is too much to actually exit the car and open the passenger door in order to scoop the contents back in the school bag, so I twist my left shoulder back and rotate my arm out of its socket for the sake of saving the embarrassment. I manage to shove in the two pencil cases (not zipped up), three packets of Blu Tack, one half-eaten Digestive caramel biscuit (which she didn't ask permission to take to school), four pieces of homework that have never been given in and a reading diary that has lost its back cover because the puppy has chewed it. I hand over the bag, minus a few 'fwendship' cards saying BFF – with names crossed out and others inserted. The daughter grunts at me and I wonder why I am the mother who never has their departing child saying, 'I love you Mumma.' She turns on her heels and says, 'Don't forget a snack when you pick me up.'

The PE teacher is eyeballing me to move on, again. The Against All Odds Girl doesn't close the car door. I rotate my arm the other way out of its socket because again I can't bear the shame of leaving the car to close the door (I am English and would rather go to A&E than do that). My arm is now aching, and muscles are mostly probably sprained. I don't think I can give the speedometer the bird that I want to because it hurts so much. Some of the items from the bag are rolling around the car mats, alongside other mouldy items from 2006, when the Teenager arrived.

It's quickly the evening and I turn my attentions to the Middle Child, who is doing a Design and Technology project. He has chosen William Morris and wants to build a miniature house with some of the designer's fabric curtains. The Against All Odds Girl can't help herself with the craft excitement and the rarity of a brother that will indulge in being over the top about getting a shoe box and turning it into a mansion. She begins to remove items from the doll's house that she never uses and stuff the shoe box with patterned armchairs from the 1970s (heirloom treasures, init). The Middle Child prints off Morris wallpaper, except he can't work out how to zoom it out, so we have several print outs that are ever so tiny and therefore have to be cut and plastered on with glue that no longer sticks because children have left the tops off. So, Sellotape is also needed, and I must find the end of it a million times, while pretending to smile, unlike the speedometer.

They get bored because that's what children do - or maybe just mine - and *Countryfile* is on, with someone showcasing a sheepdog, which is more interesting than the mini wallpaper that won't stick to the Adidas box. I finish the project because I am a perfectionist and need to get an A**. The children are lying on the sofa, watching a dog obediently do its work, while I wonder how it is that middle age is about doing your child's homework, having cooked them dinner and paid for the shiny shoes in the box that you are now turning into a miniature world.

Still, there's always the school pick-up to cheer you up. They have decided that as well as the sad face shame of driving too fast you now also must wear a mask, so you can't speak to anyone. It's like a daily casting of *Contagion* and in my version, I can't see either because my breath is re-routed by the mask I am asked to wear and is steaming up my glasses. I am now engaging my other senses, notably hearing, to identify whether it's the Against All Odds Girl I am shuffling into the car or someone else's darling.

Thankfully, the voice is booming. I also know it's her because I can smell the clandestine caramel biscuits, lingering on her school uniform. She asks why I look so glum. I point at the plague scene and the glasses that I can't see out of. 'Never mind, Mum,' she says, 'If you wear a mask in the car then you won't see the sad face each day.'

Hospitals filling up – Tabitha Peters, aged 12

19 November, 2020 – Living the American Dream

The Oxford University COVID vaccine is reported to show a strong immune response in those in their 60s and 70s, something researchers have described as 'encouraging'.

Researchers in the UK and Netherlands have found that tocilizumab, a drug used to treat rheumatoid arthritis, shows promising signs of being able to treat critically ill COVID patients in trials.

Israel, Sri Lanka, Namibia, Rwanda, the US Virgin Islands, Uruguay, Bonaire, St Eustatius and Saba and the Northern Mariana Islands are all added to the UK's quarantine exemption list. No countries are removed from the list.

Fashion retailers Peacocks and Jaeger go into administration after their owners, Edinburgh Woollen Mill Group, fails to find a buyer, risking 4,700 jobs.

The UK government announces £300m of emergency funding for sports impacted by the absence of spectators.

First Minister of Scotland, Nicola Sturgeon, says that governments across the UK face a 'difficult balance' over how to approach Christmas.

(Wikipedia, 2020)

The Against All Odds Girl is moving to the US with her 'fwends' to stay in a mansion that has a spa and an inbuilt sweet shop. It is a well-rehearsed announcement that occurs between mouthfuls of salt and vinegar Walkers crisps and the fiddling of the volume button on the radio at 4.10pm, on the drive back from school.

We arrive home as I contemplate the American Dream that awaits my daughter; she turns on her heels, buoyed by the knowledge that the hard part is over, and she has 'told' me. 'OK,' I say. 'Well I hope you'll be happy, and I suppose I must let you go if that's how you feel.' She sucks her breath in between instalments of *The Next Step*, which, although actually Canadian, not American, is perhaps one of the places where the dreaming began. It's a tween/teen dance school drama and the Against All Odds Girl and the girlfriends imagine themselves living in a palace where they 'high kick' all day and go to a smoothie bar to 'chat' about their dance routines.

Eldon, who has blonde hair and is about 12, has just declared his love to another dancer. The Against All Odds Girl looks dewy-eyed up at him, but says, 'Actually Mummy, I think I'll miss you too much.' She places her hand on her hips as she flicks her hair, trying to portray this as another well-considered thought.

'OK,' I say, 'But if you need to go, then that's what you should do,' enjoying the make-believe game as much as her, because who doesn't like a yoghurt drink and one fewer child in their house?

'I'll just have to tell the girls in the morning,' she says while biting her lip and flirting with the drama of the big announcement she must deliver before morning registration. 'Well, it's up to you, I mean it's sad but maybe it's for the best,' I reply.

'Yes,' she says, 'Because I don't really know where America is and that person, Donald Trump – that's the one, isn't it, Mummy? Well isn't he refusing to leave and so maybe he won't let us come, anyway,' she says, as she watches Eldon plant a kiss on his new crush.

'Well there you go, darling; just tell the girls you can't go because the man with the orange tan says you can't.'

'OK, good,' she concludes, and I see her forehead relax as the worry of the emigration eases.

Meanwhile the Teenager is coveting a 'mechanical keyboard'. I thought everything IT related was already so. He asks at dinner if he can use the generous Amazon voucher his godmother has given him for this reason.

'Well, I'd rather you think about it because that's a lot of money and you might change your mind.'

'But it's my money,' he says while twirling his spaghetti in a furious anti-clockwise motion. I look at the Husband for support, but he is currently giving himself seconds and abstaining from hardcore parenting in favour of food consumption, so that I am solely the bad cop of keyboards.

'Mum, I really don't understand why I can't spend my money how I want.'

'Because,' I say, 'You need to consider using your money wisely. For example, I really want this pair of trainers, but they are a lot of money, so I have been thinking about them for over a year.' (That's not entirely true but sometimes a month feels like a year, right?)

'Well that's just silly, Mum, just get them if you want to.'

The cogs start turning in my head, helpfully oiled by the carb hit of the spag bol and I begin to think he is a genius. 'Well, yes, perhaps I should get those trainers, but the point is do I need the trainers?' (I hope he says yes because I also need validation over my consumer choices – it's a kinda reverse psychology that is going on.)

'Do it Mum, life is too short,' - an expression he has heard me say a million times when wanting the Husband to pour me another glass of the lady fuel.

'OK, well maybe I will,' I say, because I now have both the nod to buy the trainers and the excuse that the Husband didn't back me when I tried to do the right thing and tell the Teenager not to splash the cash.

The next day, after the Against All Odds Girl has delivered the blow to the girls that they won't be going to the US because the man with the tan has outlawed it, an email drops into my inbox from the Teenager.

'I've ordered it, Mum, because it was on special offer. So now, I have saved money. Thanks, Mum, I love you.' I make a note to use one of these strap lines with the pasta-eating Husband, when I buy the trainers, because who can be cross about a bargain?

Jay – Oli Manson, aged 6

26 November, 2020 – Coloured Face Masks and DNA Checks

England's new tier system is announced, to come into force on 2 December. Most of the country, including London and Liverpool, will be Tier 2, while large parts of the Midlands, North East and North West, including Greater Manchester and Birmingham, will be in Tier 3. Only the Isle of Wight, Cornwall and the Isles of Scilly will be in Tier 1.

Media question the efficiency of the University of Oxford/AstraZeneca vaccine, since a preliminary report combined results from two trials, which used different doses.

(Wikipedia, 2020)

The Against All Odds Girl is clutching some pink tinsel with butterflies flying out of it. She is decorating her desk at school with the purchase that she forced upon me, in November. I don't agree with the early onset of Christmas or the colour of the tinsel because I am a traditionalist at heart and tinsel is silver or red. Her stubbornness is a kind of homage to uniqueness as well as her ability to research Amazon for items that I find hideous and offensive. She is stroking it as we try to outwit the school speedometer; we cross the line and it's still on a sad face. The anxiety it triggers causes her to stroke the pink offensiveness more violently because she is compliant about a lot of things - just not homeschooling - and so the morose face doesn't sit well with her general attitude towards doing the right thing.

She shouts, 'Slow down,' while refusing to remove her hand from the light blush colour of the decoration. I can see that she doesn't feel comfortable with not being able to add a hand gesticulation but it's choices, init, so you can't covet your latest merchandise and tell your mother to stop speeding by waving your hands. She climbs out at the drive-through, where you don't get a Quarter Pounder, either with cheese or not. She is still clutching the tinsel while also holding her school bag, water bottle and spare trainers for cross country. 'Have a good day,' I say while trying not to beam too much as she waltzes off with all her items as I do the 'hell yeah, you can have her for a few hours,' dance of joy in my head.

The Middle Child has lost his school face masks. They are dished out in pairs. He has lost both. I wonder if they are with the digital pens or someone at his school is making a packet out of selling on all these items that we continuously buy. 'Can you buy me some more?' he asks. 'Your brother has a spare,' I say pointing at the one that is hanging off a bronze duck that is a water jug but has a better use and temporary secondment in COVID times as a place to hang face masks. 'Oh, Mum, you really don't understand, do you? Year 7 has the school name in white and his is in orange.' 'Really?' I say with incredulity because surely this can't be possible. Why do they have to have different coloured logos? Isn't it complicated enough? Now siblings can't share masks. 'Well no one will notice,' I say, raising an eyebrow at both the bronze duck and him.

'They will and it's not right.' I wonder when my children became so compliant about speeding and coloured logos on face masks.

Just as I start to consider checking their DNA and whether they can be my children on account of their lawfulness, the Teenager says he saw his brother in geography, when he was walking to his saxophone lesson. 'Shouldn't you have been in lessons when your brother was beginning his geo?' I ask. 'Mum, I left the maths unit test early because I couldn't do it, so I said I had to get to my sax lesson. I walked slowly.' Colour fills my cheeks again because I know at least one of my three is of my blood line. 'Fair enough,' I say, as the Teenager gives me a nod in a rare moment of solidarity.

I add 'face masks' to the list of things to buy, along with an outdoor gazebo because the only sniff of a social life these days is sitting in the cold with your party of six or going for a dog walk. Even the new puppy is raising her eyes at me when I announce yet another walkies with another friend and their different type of dog, but you have to take whatever you can get in these times, which is never a fast-food fix on the school drive-by or a coffee or wine with your mummy friends at 9am, after you have dropped the darlings off. I am considering re-branding my WhatsApp groups by dog walk routes because there's never an invitation to anything but a traipse around a local copse.

The tier system – the Against All Odds Girl, aged 8

DECEMBER, 2020

3 December, 2020 – Quarantined Christmas Cards and Highlighter Pens

The number of recorded COVID-related deaths in the UK passes 60,000 after a further 414 deaths take the total to 60,113.

Dr Anthony Fauci, the leading infectious disease expert in the United States, criticises the UK's approval process for the Pfizer/BioNTech vaccine, suggesting it has not been as rigorous as that of the US. In defence the UK says the vaccination is safe and effective. Fauci later retracts his statement and apologises for the comments.

England's deputy chief medical officer, Jonathan Van-Tam, says that the first wave of vaccines could cut the number of hospitalisations and deaths in England by 99%.

After some ministers suggest that Brexit speeded up the process allowing the UK to get the vaccine first, Education Secretary, Gavin Williamson, responds by saying that the UK got the vaccine first because it is a 'much better country' with superior medical experts.

The first batch of the Pfizer/BioNTech vaccine arrives in the UK and is stored at an undisclosed location ready for distribution to hospitals and vaccination centres around the country.

The student travel window opens, allowing them to return home from university for Christmas.

Supermarket retailer ASDA announces plans to repay £340m of business rates relief to the government, joining Tesco, Sainsbury's, Morrisons and Aldi, which have made similar announcements, meaning £1.7bn of rates relief is to be repaid.

(Wikipedia, 2020)

The Against All Odds Girl's Christmas cards have been put into quarantine. She smirks at me with a, 'I told you so,' followed by, 'Why don't you read your emails from the school?' There is no thanks, however, for getting the flipping cards which involved a special trip to the supermarket that has an orange logo like Donald Trump's tan. There is also no pat on the back for then purchasing the silver chocolate coins to go inside them that are apportioned according to popularity and whether you are in the girl club (2) or the boy club (1).

'I don't read all the emails from school,' I say while waving my hands like an air hostess at the piles of washing, dirty plates and general detritus, hoping that is a reasonable explanation as to why.

'But you read all your WhatsApps,' she says, flicking her hair and snarling.

'Well, erm, yes possibly I do but it's kind of like you not wanting to do your homework and instead watching someone make slime on YouTube.'

'Not really, Mum. Sometimes you must read the letter, like when it says you can't bring your cards in for 72 hours after they have been written.'

'And sometimes you have to do your homework for the day when it is due and not leave it in your bag for an entire week,' I say in smug defiance. I can do 'matchy, matchy' too. The pupils in her eyes are getting bigger, which generally means I really am in trouble.

'The thing is, Mum, I am not causing a health pandemic if I don't do my homework, but I am if you don't read the letter and take the cards in without sealing them up for the number of hours it says.'

I wonder how it has happened that my eight-year-old daughter has morphed into Matt Hancock and outwitted me in the exchange of priority morals.

The Teenager is on a week of end-of-term exams. He is 'sweating' it with the books as he says. I don't really know what this means apart from a term that he throws at me about being what I would have called a 'spod' in my day. The 2020 teenage version of the word is about perspiration and hard work in bizarre union.

'It's just the chem, Mum,' he says, while flicking through Instagram and looking misty-eyed at people who have better lives and who aren't revising.

'So, I suggest you revise that then as a priority,' I say, as the Against All Odds Girl raises her eyebrows at me ranking things by importance.

'Why don't you get a highlighter and do a mind map about the periodic table,' I say. He looks up briefly from one of his social media pals, who is trying to look cool in a facemask while on the bus, and says, 'You don't need to do that, Mum, you just do it in your head.' I am now 'sweating', but not from hard work but because I am genuinely concerned about how the teenagers of today revise for exams without either a luminous green or a fluorescent pink highlighter.

'But you are not writing anything down,' I say, my eyes now popping out on storks a bit like the new puppy, who has just seen the Husband carry in a box of pigs' ears for her. 'Mum, listen, you don't need to, I am just reading it over and getting it in my head.'

'Well why don't you just try; I'll get you a highlighter shall I?' I have no idea if we have a highlighter despite having bought at least 100 since the children were born. I mean what does happen to all the stationery purchases? We have invested several hundreds of pounds over the years but there isn't any evidence of that.

'Seriously, Mum, just stop sweating about it,' he says as the dog nods in agreement and begins to chew another animal's ear off.

The Middle Child pitches in with a curve ball to say he is off to a karaoke night with his school friends. 'Nice I say,' as I prioritise the WhatsApp group of my pals to arrange some Christmas drinks (because I want to relish in socialising too) outside in December with thermals and a padded jacket on - although we are going to have to choose to kill someone because you can only have six. 'Well, I am not using your stupid highlighter,' the Teenager says and I just reply, 'OK,' because I can't find one, anyhow, and I have to spend some time 'prioritising' whom to sack off from the social gathering where seven is a 'no no'.

Vaccine arrival – Tabitha Peters, aged 12

27 December, 2020 – Christmas Special: Tier 4 Stylee

Speaking to The Sunday Times, Pascal Soriot, chief executive of AstraZeneca, says they have found a 'winning formula' with the Oxford/AstraZeneca vaccine. Sources, including ITV News, report that the vaccine will be approved for use in the UK within days.

The B117 strain of COVID, the presence of which was first detected in the UK, has now been identified in a number of other countries, including Australia.

(Wikipedia, 2020)

The children wonder why Father Christmas has been to Primark and gone for functional stocking items: pants, socks, T-shirts. The Middle Child looks quizzically at me and asks why he didn't get the headphones that he asked for in the letter to Santa that he chucked in the chimney on Christmas Eve. I explain that the elves at the North Pole need a little more notice. He replies, 'Doesn't Amazon Prime deliver overnight?' The Against All Odds Girl runs her hands through her hair and says, 'It's not from Amazon stupid, it's from Father Christmas.' She is rejoicing in the letter for the 'speshall necklace and sweet hamper' (too much time at Fortnum's) that she has asked for … in good time. I am joyful in the fact that the practical socks may mean the boys actually wear them (in addition to the fact that they no longer believe, meaning I no longer have to explain away the absence of expensive items that I am not prepared to assign thanks for to the man at the North Pole). It also means that I don't have to sort out the sock pile because I have learnt that if it has never happened in COVID time, it really is never going to happen. So, best just to go with the quick route on that one and throw that job in the bin.

There are no grandparents, or aunts and uncles, or cousins to adorn our Christmas table, so we have brought the chickens in, who are also locked up due to bird flu, to join us – BoJo didn't say anything about poultry having to be dead to join you in the kitchen, so what's the difference? We are very food chain aware at the moment - they have come to eat the left-over turkey, split with the puppy, who is also trying a Brussels sprout and swilling it around her mouth in the hope that like for us humans, it may get better if you combine it with gravy. The chickens are now eating the bird that is their senior, while the puppy is having a turn at the pork stuffing because she wants in on the act of eating animals that are bigger than you are.

It's a Christmas of vouchers: Waterstones (have you met my children, they don't read anything but the *Beano* or the many badly spelt WhatsApp messages they get?); Amazon (someone couldn't be bothered to think or ask); but the Christmas present of the year goes to the great aunt who has tried very, very hard with a medley of gifts for the Against All Odds Girl, including a Santa hairband all-in-one that looks a bit like a budgie smuggler intended for a singleton spending Christmas home-alone.

Our Christmas present to the three children involves a trip to the boundaries of Tier 4 to collect a pool table that the Husband got from an auction. In the picture it is propped up against a wall. He phones from the pick-up, which is a covert mission. 'Hi. There's good news and bad.' 'OK,' I say, as I raise my eyebrows, while trying to buoy up enthusiasm for dressing a Christmas table that will have the same people sitting at it as the night before, and the night before that … since February.

'What is it?' I ask. 'Well, we've got the pool table and it fits in the car.' (This plan involved a separate decision-making process of whether to hire a white van to collect the item but the Husband wondered if he would be mistakenly caught in a pile-up headed to Dover with some other truckers trying to get home for Christmas.) 'OK, that's good,' I say, placing the crackers at an angle to try and make it look as though I am bothering. 'Well, the bad news is that it doesn't have any legs.' 'Sorry,' I say, as I slide into the reality of COVID Christmas and realise that none of the children would be bothered if I delivered a McDonald's on their laps for Christmas lunch.

'I did wonder if it was propped up on its side because there weren't any legs. Right, this is the last time we buy something online without seeing it.' 'What, like the puppy?' he says, whose bad behaviour he blames on her being bought from a dodgy dog breeder, who may have stolen other puppy photos from bona fide peeps for the purposes of flogging her bad ones. 'Let's not go there,' I say.

I am wondering if it is possible to play pool on the floor, or if the puppy will just pee all over it, as with everything else – or, worse, do a poo on it, which is her party trick when you don't give her any attention. I start to drag through a table surplus to requirements, like the third child who doesn't fit the sensible family model of two adults, two children.

The Middle Child is helping me, while sucking a candy stick where you snip the top off and inhale the contents and then apparently chuck the top on the floor.

We can't get the legs out of the narrow door so now I am heaving most of the weight of it on my own and the Middle Child looks bored. We agree to abandon it, just as the Husband appears. He moves it easily and glances over with 'a what is all the fuss about?' look as I rub my back, which is now hurting. We lift the pool table (sans jambes); it's a Christmas of turkey crowns, where legs are outlawed. The table sits at a slant, so the Husband levers it into position with two bits of wood. The children start to play, while the adult nerves are on edge that it's going to end up on the floor or someone's toes (but at least they are covered with socks). The wine helps. We add in an insurance, some of the plastic vouchers from bookstores that won't be spent, to prop it up - so at least they now serve a purpose.

It's a few days later and the novelty has worn off. The children have crept back to the screens and the pool table without the legs is being used as resting place for discarded sweet wrappers and chocolate boxes.

No Christmas for us – Sophie Williams, aged 12

JANUARY, 2021

4 January, 2021 – School's Closed, Init: Groundhog Day

Brian Pinker, 82, becomes the first person to receive the Oxford/AstraZeneca COVID vaccine, as vaccinations using the vaccine begin in the UK.

Margaret Ferrier, the MP for Rutherglen and Hamilton West, is arrested by Scottish police and charged in connection with 'alleged culpable and reckless conduct' for using public transport while experiencing COVID symptoms.

Prime Minister, Boris Johnson, later confirms that England will enter a third lockdown from 5 January, with similar restrictions to the first lockdown in March 2020, including school closures - unlike the second lockdown in November - to all pupils except for children of keyworkers and vulnerable children.

The UK's chief medical officers recommend the COVID alert level is moved from level four to level five.

(Wikipedia, 2021)

Hell hath no fury like a mother with a school on the blink of closure and a teenager still in bed at 11.06am. It's the day before the day before the Against All Odds Girl is due back to the building marked 'primary school, please step inside'. Except the school is in Essex and it's a game of dominoes, where a chief at the council has said, 'Shut it, shut it, shut it.' If you throw a stone over to the school across the field in Suffolk, however, the overlord at the council there says, 'Open it, open it, open it.' Sod's law goes like this: you have two boys at secondary school in Suffolk, where their return to school is delayed until 18 January (but where primary schools are open); you also have one daughter at a primary school in Essex, which is open according to the government, but may be closed because councils have more say then BoJo. Result = no children are going to any school soon because your children are either the wrong age or live in the wrong county.

I am trying to be wholesome but failing. I suggest that while we await the final nail in the coffin of what we know will be 'the computer says no' to the school being open, we draw a dot-to-dot. The Against All Odds Girl asks, 'What is this?' 'You know,' I say, 'You connect the dots and see what picture it makes.' She looks at me while tapping her new Smiggle highlighter, which promises to smell of watermelon but is more like the scent of someone who has tried to clear up vomit with disinfectant. 'It has 562 dots.' 'Isn't that exciting,' I say, knowing already by the venom in her eyes that the lack of instant gratification that the 'yoof' of today buzz off won't wash with this one.

'I used to spend my childhood doing things like that,' I say. 'Yes, Mum, but you also thought puzzles with lots of bits were exciting and they're not,' she replies, swapping the fruit inhalation for a vanilla fix. 'Anyhow, it's a seahorse,' she snarls at me, high with the intoxication of highlighters that waft sick fumes at you.

I tell the children they need to spend time on tasks that require concentration and focus because they will get more satisfaction from that. I say this as I scroll through Instagram because I need my own 'fix' of dopamine and it's OK to be a hypocrite when you are a mother. The Teenager is responding to instant gratification with his own time vacuum and appears. 'Morning,' I say, asking the Against All Odds Girl to read out the digital time from her Smiggle watch (we have invested heavily in someone that has been clever enough to drug children with smelly stationery). 'It's 11.06, Mum.'

'Yes, it is,' I say looking at the Teenager who had promised to do some chemistry revision on compounds but has found sleep is more important. 'I need my zzzzz, Mum,' he says, clearly too tired to even contemplate getting a bowl and spoon for breakfast out, let alone learn the formula for ammonium chloride. 'Well, it's lunchtime in an hour and a half so perhaps you ought to catch up,' I say. 'What's the problem? It's the holidays.' 'Yes, it is, although the holidays go on and on, particularly during COVID and so perhaps you ought to try and get up earlier.' 'No,' he says and the Against All Odds Girl shouts, 'It's now 11.09.' The Big Ben with the flicky hair looks triumphant, as the Teenager gesticulates a 'I don't care' with his hands.

The Middle Child has befriended his sister to get more Xbox time because I am limiting Fortnite. 'It's OK, I'll play with her; she wants to play Rocket League.' OK, it's not shooting I suppose but it is 11 o'clock, erm I mean 11.09. 'I suppose it's better than the other game, but shouldn't we be doing something like Lego, mid-morning?' They both look at me with a similar look to the one when I suggested the dot-to-dot.

The parent WhatsApp group has gone wild about school closures. Everyone is trying to be 'apolitical' while really wanting to belt Gavin Williamson with one of my stones that I am not good at throwing. I am scanning the messages and wondering whether to pull the children off the Xbox or use the babysitting time to pack away the Christmas decorations.

The Husband has put us on dry January, just to complete the moroseness. I am crossing off the days (with a pencil that doesn't smell) of the vile month, in which you pretend orange squash is a winner. Let's face it, there have only been four of them – 27 to go until the time I can relish in wine o'clock again. I am wondering where the genius is in being sober when you may have to homeschool until spring, and I reckon I may have to step into the Teenager's time vacuum and not pay heed to days or times and make them up to suit myself. Still there's always the dot-to-dot to complete but she's right, it is a seahorse and the next page is a whale, so why bother?

Go to school, don't go to school – Tabitha Peters, aged 12

8 January, 2021 – Homeschool: Lockdown 1, Erm No Lockdown 2, Erm No Lockdown 3

The Moderna vaccine becomes the third COVID vaccine to be given approval for use in the UK.

Sadiq Khan, the Mayor of London, declares a 'major incident' in London, where he says COVID is 'out of control'.

Research from the COVID Symptom Study suggests COVID cases increased by a third in the UK and reached 70,000 new cases a day between 26 December and 3 January, while the Office for National Statistics estimates 1.2 million people had COVID over the same time period.

The R number is estimated to be between 1.0 and 1.4.

The UK records its largest number of daily COVID-related deaths so far, with 1,325 new deaths, bringing the total to 79,833. The figure surpasses 21 April 2020, when there were 1,224 deaths. However, average deaths are estimated to be two thirds of the peak in April, suggesting the high daily total may have occurred as a result of a backlog in reporting deaths over the Christmas period.

Education Secretary, Gavin Williamson, announces that GCSE and A-Level exams in England this summer will be replaced by teacher assessments, telling MPs he would 'trust in teachers rather than algorithms'.

An England-wide advertising campaign launches on television, fronted by Chief Medical Officer, Chris Whitty, urging people to stay at home and act as though they have COVID.

(Wikipedia, 2021)

It feels wrong to eat poached eggs on toast, with a side of Jaffa cakes, when your son is in a French lesson and translating: 'For lunch, we eat chicken with green beans.' He is pointing to my lunch and mouthing 'hungry' to me and showing me up that I am eating biscuits and not haricots verts. We are spreading out because the Middle Child can't tolerate sharing the same room as the Teenager who he complains is 'stretching' and/or 'yawning' too much. (There's no pleasing some, or any.) The new workspace is the kitchen table and he is propping up his laptop with a bottle of red-hot chilli sauce, while muting his Teams meeting to shoo me away to collect blank paper for his art lesson. I am like a PA to the children, but without an attractive salary, holiday allowance or chef du jour.

It's Friday afternoon and the Teenager is scheduled for CCF (Combined Cadet Force). Obvs there is no army uniform in sight or military march to comply with, so he is doing 'exercise' in the kitchen, which the Middle Child is occupying, while participating in a fractions lesson and watching his older brother's bottom in his face, as he attempts to do squats to the smiling PE assassin, who is on mute because of the Middle Child's maths. The puppy is looking bemused in her crate at the derrieres and art/maths attempts but not complaining, because she is on about six meals a day, due to a lack of ownership of who feeds her.

The Against All Odds Girl is at 'skool, skool' because I am a 'key worker' (like carpet-fitters in hospitals) teaching the children of 'key workers' (oh the irony and eligibility criteria). My part-time job (which usually takes a heavy two mornings per week and couples with the client writing), like all good part-time jobs, is actually full-time because all the staff have COVID or are at a centre finding out if they have it. When my colleague also calls in absent because she is off for a 'flu jab', I tell her, 'That is so 80s.' I pick up the girl with the venom in her eyes from the 'skool, skool' and ask how it has gone, she replies, 'Good,' when in earshot of the teacher, which is downgraded in the car to 'OK,' because she is missing her 'fwends' who are getting to 'keep it real' at their homesteads and who only have to dress in uniform up to their waists.

'Do you want to go tomorrow?' I ask, pitching it as optional when I know it isn't, I am in to reverse psychology and am confident this will play out in my favour. 'Only if you give me Pringles in my packed lunch.' 'Done,' I say, and we move on to more important things like which Smiggle highlighter she got high on today.

Of course, the house of homeschooling boys and remote-working husband find it impossible to do any household chores while doing their day jobs. They are existing in a bachelor pad in which they spend their time eating crisps at their desks, looking for pencils that are sharp and WhatsApping their mates when the drivel of the Teams gets too much. The Against All Odds Girl and I open the front door and declare the tsunami of detritus a 'disgrace'. The Teenager looks up from the squats and the Middle Child from finding out what a seventh of 49 is, while the Husband hands me three coffee cups and a dirty plate. 'Too busy,' they mouth as we set down our packed lunches, minus the 'bribery' Pringle crisps. 'Right,' I say (when what I mean is bleep, bleep, expletive, expletive), 'What did you do at lunchtime? Couldn't you have cleaned the kitchen and put the dishwasher on?' The Teenager finishes the final squat while doing a comedy Mexican wave. 'We watched *Death in Paradise*.' 'Great,' I say, wondering whether swapping Fortnite for murders on a beach is any better or indeed a reasonable excuse for not helping domestically.

I make a stand and declare, 'I am not doing it,' (they know from history this is not true but I go with it anyway). 'I'm going for a run; do you want to come?' I say to the Husband, who is also muting his call.

'No.' 'Great,' I think, finally a time when I can be alone rather than surrounded by people that give me dirty crockery or either stand with me while I am having a pee or shout at me from another room when I am in the bathroom (finally alone). I set off with my old friends, the *Pet Shop Boys*, because I am also thinking, like my colleague, that the 80s is where it's at, a time when: you spoke to people; you hugged them; you didn't have to learn another language aged 11 while watching your mother eat poached eggs; Friday activities weren't bottom squats while your brother did maths and your father thumped on the ceiling because he was also on Teams; the puppy didn't have to sign up to weight watchers because she was being fed by five people at each meal; you didn't have to lie to get your kid to school on the basis that you did something ever so important like operating the sewers or being an Uber cab driver with nowhere to drive to. I put on my shoes and tune in to *What Have I Done To Deserve This?* and look around hoping that there is no child, husband, pupil or hound following me.

Siskin – Oli Manson, aged 6

15 January, 2021 – Dry Jan and Hiding From the Geo Teacher

The R number is estimated to be between 1.2 and 1.3, a fall on the previous week, with data also suggesting there are signs the number of COVID cases are beginning to fall.

Prime Minister, Boris Johnson, announces that the UK will close all travel corridors from Monday 18 January to 'protect against the risk of as yet unidentified new COVID strains', and meaning that anyone travelling to the UK will need to provide a negative COVID test before embarking on their journey.

Following a ruling by the Supreme Court, tens of thousands of small businesses will receive insurance payments covering losses accrued during the first lockdown of March 2020.

(Wikipedia, 2021)

I am participating in an 11-year-old's geography class, about Earth. The Middle Child has taken a 'comfort' break and I am his replacement. I put the earphones in and look at the teacher, who has a background of a desert with some trees dotted about. What I don't know is that the pupil, who I am now impersonating (badly) has pressed the hand waving button to ask a question. He is no longer here, as you know, because he is peeing in my house (somewhere). The teacher, who is in the Gobi Desert says, 'Middle Child, do you want to say something?' (Well obvs she doesn't say MC, but I am in to data protection, so you need to bear with me.) I have no idea what to do. He could be at any one of our three 'comfort' rooms so I either play Russian roulette and run to get him and win without an interminable pause or I go to the wrong one and she will think he is incapable of asking an intelligent question or, even worse, speaking at all.

The other option is that I try to pitch my voice into that of an 11-year-old boy's and ask something sensible about the 'journey to the Earth', which again and obvs I have no idea about, apart from perhaps throwing one out there with, 'It looks a bit like an apple core,' but I think that's a bit too reception class like and the rest of the pupils may laugh (at me, who they think is him). I may crack under the pressure and reveal my identity, together with my lack of geography knowledge. I decide to do none of these things and slide down the chair and hide.

It's a cracking look for a 45-year-old mother of three and certainly channels the 'in control' vibe I am pretending to convey most of the time. The Middle Child appears, zipping up his trousers, and snatches the headphones off me, 'What is the temperature at the centre, Miss?' I am still under the table, minus the headphones, which I'd like to add are mine.

He is now resting his foot on me as I get familiar with a piece of chicken tikka that hasn't made it into the bin. My nose is slightly pressed on top of it and I have one of those moments when I consider licking it before I am 'brought back into the room of adulthood' and realise that even though no one is watching, except the puppy, this is scraping the barrel of my extremely low standards of acceptability. I berate myself for knowing nothing about the planet on which I have lived for almost half a century, as well as being so incapable of sweeping up crumbs from under the kitchen table, as well as having sinful thoughts about eating them.

The Against All Odds Girl is learning spellings. Among them are 'ruin', 'truth' and 'fluid'. It's defo a case of terms for 2020 and now 2021, too – because the 'truth' is that we are all 'ruined' unless we have a shot of 'fluid' vaccine in our arms. I consider phoning the teacher and telling her she should add 'pig sticking' (my sister's term for us all getting the jab, it makes me laugh) and 'variant' in for good measure.

It's a good job she is familiar with these words because her grandfather has been waiting in a makeshift vaccination centre held up with some brown tape and tarpaulin, which is one of the tests you have to pass (do you want it enough to sit in sub-zero temperatures?) before you can get your shot of Pfizer. He WhatsApps me on the 'Pasties and other things' group - 'Got it. It did not hurt. Ticket number 378!' - together with a photo of the vac centre with the blue oilcloth.

The Teenager is studying *The Taming of the Shrew*. There are various chats appearing on the message board to the teacher. An academic one: 'Sir, I am confused as to the difference between Petruchio and Lucentio,' (points for knowing the names of two characters). The rest fall under the category of 'practical': 'Sorry, Sir, I was late I was having lunch because I'm in school,' (you have to eat); 'I've read it and I don't understand any of it,' (fair enough); 'Sir, what are we doing?' (again, fair); 'I had some problems with the WiFi,' (someone has been asleep). The Teenager is googling SparkNotes, which I would also file under 'fair' but also possibly 'needs to try harder'.

I'm halfway through dry January, which let me tell you is about as fun as a poke in the eye with a hot stick (not a pig one). I have started hoovering at 10pm at night because there is literally no joy in downing several tonic waters sans the gin. The Against All Odds Girl is in a mood about this, as well as the spellings, because she says it is keeping her awake (not the re-run of R-U-I-N but the low hum of the vac – not the pig sticking one, the one that sweeps up chicken tikka and the like). To be fair, it's that plus the puppy, who keeps escaping the baby gate and running up the stairs to jump on her head. It's another 'fair' point but I cannot do anything about this new late-night cleaning habit until I have replaced it with the joy of the 'support bubbles' that come from a glass vessel marked 'prosecco'.

Dreaming of seeing loved ones – Tabitha Peters, aged 12

22 January, 2021 – Bridgerton and GCSE options

The R number is estimated to be between 0.8 and 1, meaning the epidemic is shrinking, while Office for National Statistics suggests infection levels have either plateaued or are beginning to decline.

At a Downing Street press conference, Prime Minister, Boris Johnson, says early evidence suggests the new COVID variant discovered in the UK may have a higher mortality rate, but that there is huge uncertainty over the figures and vaccination is expected to work.

The release date of the 25th James Bond film, 'No Time to Die', is delayed for a third time because of the COVID outbreak and will now debut on 8 October 2021.

The UK government launches its 'Can you look them in the eyes?' campaign, featuring doctors, healthcare workers and COVID patients, urging people not to leave home unless for essential reasons.

(Wikipedia, 2021)

The Middle Child is studying African tribal patterns. I say, 'What's that for?' He replies, 'To learn about the wider world,' with a 'dah' look as if I obviously don't know anything about the planet in which we live because I am not familiar with squiggly lines that denote enlightenment. I tap my finger and say, the only pattern you need to know is: 'Hands, face, space.' I add, 'Another pattern is that your hair grows, you cut it and it grows again.' He runs his fingers (hopefully washed due to the slogan, but probably not) through his gold locks because I told him yesterday that he is beginning to look like Liam Gallagher, who he then googles (because he has no idea why I find this comparison funny) and argues the toss that he does not.

The Teenager, whose hair is OK because he let the Husband cut it in a negotiation for more Xbox time, has asked me to wash his bed sheets. I am taken aback for many reasons: first, I was unaware he was 'bovvered'; secondly, this must mean I have stooped to new parenting lows. I oblige but wonder if he will notice for a few days, he doesn't, so I think all must be well in the land of teenagers and we can resume the lax cleaning efforts.

The Husband and I are supposed to be choosing the Teenager's GCSE options, I mean obviously the Teenager is selecting them, ahem, with parental input from us. I only remember the importance of this when my dear friend messages me to ask me if I have done it. 'Done what?' I ask. I'm thinking: 'changed his sheets' (how does she know?) or 'completed the car insurance' (again, how does she know?). I finally settle on the fact that she must be asking me if I have completed the *Bridgerton* series. I am poised to reply, 'Not yet, but can't wait,' when she interjects, 'GCSE choices'. 'Oh,' I say, 'When does that have to be done?' 'Half-term.'

I look at the calendar that I have specifically bought from the school, which has dates and the like of important school related events, such as the day they are supposed to tip up and the day they want you to remove the children. It's blank because the calendar person has deleted everything considering the 'hands, face, space' situation. 'Right,' I say.

I'm too embarrassed to admit that I did see that email but felt it was so important that I prioritised it to the back of my mind and catapulted the period, romance drama to the front. 'On it,' I eventually come up with because I am burning with the hypocrisy of screaming at the Teenager to pull his finger out of his proverbial and actual bottom and get out of the bed that is dirty and do some hard graft.

I am wondering if you can just do it last minute, like all good things and perhaps tick the first nine that come up on the page. I am also pondering how my parents would have handled this and then I remember that it was a bit more *Bridgerton* in their day and I would have said, 'Mother/Father [Regency, init] I have chosen my GCSE options.' They would have then said, 'That's nice dear, are you doing GCSEs, then?' They would have then driven off to the ball wearing the lovely outfits to sip the expensive champagne as in the period drama that I am obsessed with and not worried a thing about any school exams.

The puppy is looking at me as I chew this one over, as she herself swills a toy dog around her mouth. I have decided that having a puppy is about as fun as someone pouring a cup of cold sick over your head but decide to park this thought (as she is looking at me with a 'how dare you?' look) and have a quick glance at the 'Gram' to see whether other people are also choosing GCSE options or if they are baking a cake while decorating their bedroom in 'Lulworth Blue'.

I would say social media is particularly exciting at the moment and is basically a rotation of friends walking their pets and children (I am also guilty of this), posting photos of early daffodils/snowdrops or showcasing a gravity cake with smarties pouring out.

The Middle Child is finished with African patterns and is on maths in which he is answering the probability of some fella, 'Chandak', landing on one of three colours after he has spun the spinner 100 times. He whispers for some help. I have no idea, so say, 'Just put: High, medium and low,' next to the options. I lean over to the Teenager and say, 'Your enemy is apathy.' He says, 'What is apathy?' I groan and add: 'Oh, it's clear now, your GCSE options are the ones where no essays with words are required.' I say that I must go because I need to pick up the Against All Odds Girl from the 'skool, skool' because I have been working at the 'skool, skool' and remember that it is Friday, which means I have promised her a trip to the village shop to buy sweets, which basically costs 20 times as much as at the supermarket. I make a note that I will tell the Husband I bought steak for the £50, not packets of Haribo and Chocolate Oranges.

COVID variants – Tabitha Peters, aged 12

29 January, 2021 – No Screens (Again), Soggy Flapjacks, and Bye Bye to Dry Jan

Trials of the single-dose Janssen COVID-19 vaccine, of which the UK has ordered 60 million doses, have indicated it to be 66% effective, the Belgian pharmaceutical firm Janssen confirms.

Office for National Statistics figures have suggested the level of COVID cases remained stable in the week up to 23 January and may have even fallen slightly.

The R number is estimated to be between 0.7 and 1.1, but the Scientific Advisory Group for Emergencies (SAGE) warns COVID levels are still 'dangerously high'.

Amid an ongoing row over vaccine shortfalls in the European Union, the European Commission announces the introduction of controls on vaccines made in the bloc, including to Northern Ireland. Responding to the announcement, Prime Minister, Boris Johnson, says the EU must 'urgently clarify its intentions', while First Minister, Arlene Foster, describes the move as 'an incredible act of hostility'. The Commission later reverses the decision, which overrides the Northern Ireland Protocol element of the Brexit Agreement, and says that Northern Ireland will not be affected.

ITV postpones the next series of 'Britain's Got Talent' until 2022 amid concerns over safety during the COVID outbreak.

(Wikipedia, 2021)

'Do something different,' says the school: 'bake a cake,' 'go for a walk,' 'take some photos,' 'read a book,' 'make a replica of the school clock.' It is Wednesday (well, it's Friday, but who cares) and the boys' school has called in a 'no screens' afternoon because the 'screens' are creating a tech pandemic. The school, which is not open but is available online, says the screens are not good for the children, or are only good for them when they are required to be at lessons but can't be, so they have to be on the screens that are bad for them. It's a bit like parenting, when you tell the children that drinking alcohol is not good for you, and then down a glass of wine, or that reading a book is much better for wholesomeness, while you scroll through Instagram.

The children are aware of the utter hypocrisy of all the adult guidance.

The 'no screens' suggestion is so the teachers, who are weary of looking at teenagers that have initials but no face on Teams, can sit in a dark corner and rock quietly. I look at the options and suggest the following to differentiate the things that already fill their lockdown and are therefore not different.

1. 'Pick up your clothes from the floor' - before going on the walk
2. 'Clear away your plates after dinner' – before reading the book (which you haven't read up to this point, so fat chance)
3. 'Go to bed when asked' – not one hour after, or never

4. 'Go for a walk' – without groaning, moaning, or 'pretending' you have something else to do like go on a 'screen'
5. 'Get off the screen' – before jumping onto another one
6. 'Build a clock tower' – but only if you have exhausted all the other options, which you could do in reverse to make them different, but why bother?

I WhatsApp the boys at lunchtime to remind them; they immediately reply and so I scold them for being on a screen that is reminding them to not be on one.

I get home from work and hope to find a model replica of the school's Big Ben. Instead, I find mud splattered over the front door and some flapjacks that haven't formed properly. 'We did some cooking and went on a walk,' they both say triumphantly. *Death In Paradise* is on in the background, so I am slightly distracted by a beach and someone drinking a cocktail.

'I thought it was supposed to be no screens,' I say, pointing at the TV, which is channelling an island paradise where your odds of being killed are as likely as schools not opening until the summer term. 'We're multi-tasking while cooking, and the 'no screens' is the computer screen, not the TV one.' I consider looking at the small print of the school's instructions but settle on logic: 'Yes, but that's a screen and the point of the afternoon is no screens.' I am looking at the TV at this point because it's getting quite good.

‘Have a flapjack, Mum,’ says the Teenager, who is also hooked on the crime, which he shouldn’t be watching. I scoop it up with both hands and kinda snort it because it’s semi-cooked and semi-liquid.

The Middle Child lifts a cake tin lid to reveal some brownies – they look passable. He gloats about his efforts, while pointing the finger at the Teenager’s, who finds the idea of the ‘no screen’ time totally abhorrent because the pandemic has made him and everyone of his age addicted to screens. He therefore is in to cheating. So that he can get back on the screen, he quickly agrees that the brownies are better and declares that he will take a photo of the MC’s bakes, instead of his own flapjacks, and upload that to the tutor, via the screen that he is not allowed on. He announces this while shouting at the TV, ‘He did it!’

I ask why the door is covered in mud. ‘It’s because we took the puppy for a walk, like we are supposed to.’ I wonder if the ‘do something different’ means, ‘do everything the same,’ but, ‘make it dirtier’ or ‘don’t do it properly’. I consider sending in some filtered photos of flapjacks that you have to inhale before they fall apart and of the front door, which is now brown, and label them, ‘Is this different? How different is it? Do you want it to be good different? Because I think this is bad different. How about the something different is that they actually go to the actual school, rather than attend it online - which you now say they should get off. That would be different.’

The Against All Odds Girl is part of a ruse to get out of learning spellings, online. She has worked out that if you stand back at a distance when you upload your spellings (that have been tested), then they are too small to read. The teacher (who believes their angelic faces can't be capable of sabotage) gives her full points. I assume she doesn't have a magnifying glass. The daughter is pleased with her efforts because it means she can spend more time on her latest hobby, which is being a radio star. She is channelling the 'Wellerman sea shanty' and hopes that, like the postman turned TikTok pop star, the gamble will pay off and she can squirm out of academic life in favour of lyrics about tea and rum. It's something different.

It's the last weekend of January, which means it's almost the end of Dry Jan but there is no decency in this, and 1 Feb isn't until Monday and who wants to down wine or the Wellerman's rum at the start of the week? I am thinking the smart folk looked at the calendar and worked out Dry Feb was a better bet because there aren't so many days involved.

Chaffinch – Oli Manson, aged 6

FEBRUARY, 2021

5 February, 2021 – Faceplanting Between Lessons and Other Things

Captain Sir Tom Moore, who raised £32m for NHS Charities Together, dies on 2 February at the age of 100, after suffering from pneumonia and contracting COVID-19.

The R number is estimated to be between 0.7 and 1, as figures from the Office for National Statistics show evidence that COVID cases in the UK are falling.

Health Secretary, Matt Hancock, announces a target to offer all adults over the age of 50 a first COVID vaccination by May.

In a conversation with French President, Emmanuel Macron, Prime Minister, Boris Johnson, discusses collaboration between the British and French governments to tackle COVID-19.

Chancellor, Rishi Sunak, announces that small businesses will have longer to repay government sponsored loans taken out to protect them against the economic effects of the COVID-19 pandemic. The time period to repay these loans will be extended from six to ten years.

Elections for local authorities, directly elected mayors and police and crime commissioners in England and Wales are to go ahead as scheduled on 6 May, but voters will be asked to bring their own pens to the polling station.

(Wikipedia, 2021)

The Middle Child has his nose and face down on the sofa, with his legs spread either side. This is how he has been spending his break times between lessons. He occasionally moves his head to the side to see what is going on but for the majority he is just sort of lying or licking the sofa. It looks kinda relaxing, except back in parent land I worry that the upholstery has snot on it, or spit. Probably both. The Teenager chooses to spend the gaps between classes with his head snuggled into the puppy. The Against All Odds Girl mainly has her nostrils in the cake tin. It's basically all about smell and wiping your face on things, anything. I have decided that this is the difference between adults and children. The 'yoof' have no problem - and I mean no problem - with faceplanting and literally being horizontal, still or wriggling on things that may or may not be wipeable; adults do. That is my conclusion.

Homeschooling also involves minimal movement. The Teenager, when not inhaling puppy fur, moves between Teams meetings with an elbow shove. It's basically a flick of your elbow to push a dirty plate to the side (on which sat some toast that you persuaded your mother to make because you were asleep or too lazy) and then moving the other elbow to rid yourself of some scrunched up bits of paper that aren't filed and generally serve no purpose but remain on the desk every day and every hour. The physical energy required for this is minimal, as is switching on Teams. You also don't need to wear socks when you are a homeschooling teenager, since no one can see and you can't be bothered.

Once you are sockless and have done the 'elbow manoeuvre' you are then free to start your new lesson, which you time exactly, so you only flick on the screen at the exact o'clock required, not a minute before. You generally don't have a pen or pencil to hand, so you gesture to anyone in the room for an item to write with, or you just type. That works better, as you therefore don't need anything. After history and before religious studies you can do the faceplanting exercise. You don't consider taking your dirty plate to the dishwasher or doing any background reading because you are attuned to doing exactly what is comforting.

I look around the room and realise that my children are indulging in the face wipe, comfort time … again. The Middle Child looks deeply involved in the head down comfort but can quite easily move himself like a cheetah across the room to art. It's like a chameleon on heat, without the cool colours. He starts drawing an animal. The teacher says, 'Middle Child how are you getting on?' He replies, while licking some spittle off his lips (the rest is on the top of the sofa), 'I had to start again because I realised the goldfinch isn't exactly a classic African species.' I look across to his Teams, while wiping with one hand the top of the sofa. The instructions read: 'Draw an African animal.' I wonder how much clearer it must be before the Middle Child starts sketching animals from the right continent.

The Against All Odds Girl is in a ballet Zoom, which involves a few squawking girls doubling up as Darcey Bussell. The lovely ballet teacher suddenly goes into darkness as the lights turn off and texts us 'power cut, sorry'. The daughter and her band of merry 'fwends' spend their enforced break 'chatting'. This is another difference – not between adults and children but between girls and boys. Boys do not chat to their friends at break time but lie in different horizontal positions; girls feel the need to download literally everything from what they are wearing to what they may wear next or at the same time. They continue with the 'chitter chatter' in which there is no Zoom etiquette about turn-taking, so I figure they all just listen to the sound of their own voices and background their 'fwends' so it's like being at a concert when you don't actually hold a conversation but you like being part of a group that does.

I'm warming up for my first 'dwink' of the year. I know, get me and my sobriety. It's five weeks so I feel it's time, before I turn into one of those 'no thanks, just a juice' bores (sorry to those that fall under this category). I also worry that without any of the 'dwink' I may morph into my children and start faceplanting for entertainment between meals.

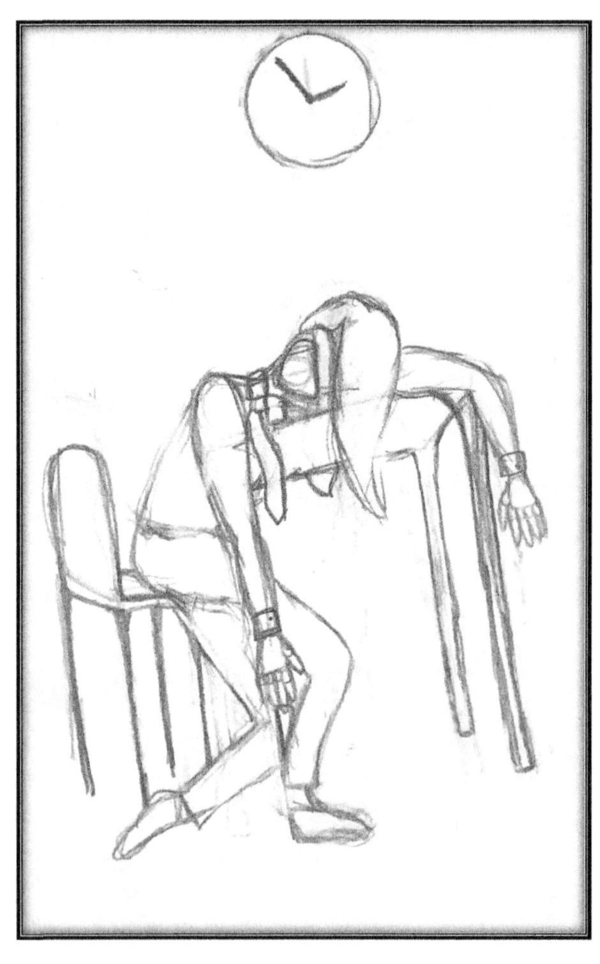

Tiresome homeschooling – Sophie Williams, 12

10 February, 2021 – Snow Day Rotation and Plastic Horses

The latest vaccination figures show that 13,058,298 people have received their first COVID vaccine; Prime Minister, Boris Johnson, urges the two million people in the first four priority groups yet to be vaccinated to 'come forward' in the coming week.

Transport Secretary, Grant Shapps, urges people not to book holidays in the UK or overseas because of COVID, saying the government does not know 'where we'll be' in the summer.

A survey of 1,500 care services suggests vaccination of care staff is lagging behind the target, with at least half of facilities having at least 30% of their staff still unvaccinated.

Elton John and Michael Caine have both featured in an ad campaign to encourage people to be vaccinated against COVID-19.

Jonathan Van-Tam, England's Deputy Chief Medical Officer, has expressed concern that uptake of COVID vaccination may not be 'as rapid or as high' among ethnic minority communities.

The World Health Organisation has recommended use of the Oxford-AstraZeneca vaccine for all adults, even in countries where new variants of the virus are prevalent.

(Wikipedia, 2021)

The Against All Odds Girl has a snow day, in which the school has made it ever so clear that you can either be on lessons or be in the snow and, if you are knee-deep in the white stuff, then you won't get blacklisted - but if you do miss the lessons then you have to live with your own guilt, that you could be considered a 'bad parent' by the parents who have put fractions before sledging.

The boys, who are at a different school, don't have a snow day because their school has decided that Monday is lessons, but that Tuesday may be a snow day. It's a carousel of snow fun in which none of the schools talk to each other, to make life as inconvenient as possible to parents.

I decide that the Against All Odds Girl shall do the maths and English lesson, which involves scribbling tenths on a whiteboard and rubbing it out with her sleeve while whispering to me that she wants a hot chocolate and that she hasn't got time to get to section C. I suppose I could help but this is lockdown 3.0 and I can't be bothered and, besides, I have a new hobby, which is selling things on Facebook Marketplace and I am slightly distracted that someone wants to come to my house to buy a toy bunk bed with a dodgy ladder and hand me cash for it. This is more thrilling than explaining that 0.2 does not mean 2.0.

I try to explain to her, while answering another call from some lady that is prepared to buy another item I am flogging - an Our Generation doll horse (if you're asking) that has a pen mark down its nose and on its bottom - that the tenths are a bit like separating the lockdown times into parts. 'Whole parts?' she asks. 'How can a whole have a part?' 'You know, it's like the horse (toy) it has parts to it that make up the whole.' 'Right,' she says, obviously not caring that a plastic horse that is departing the house has anything to do with maths.

I feel it's time to be the 'fun parent' or try to pose as one and take the girl for a sledge, while the boys continue with their lessons, which are compulsory today but not tomorrow afternoon. We walk down the lane and I ask her, 'Did you get the decimal fractions?' 'Kinda,' she says, 'Like I kinda get part of it like you said but maybe not all of it but if it's about part wholes then that's OK.' I am focusing on being in fun mum mode, so don't continue the conversation about decimal fractions because it may distract my fake smile into its more natural state of a grimace.

'Last, last sledge,' I say, which comes as easily to me as saying, 'Last, last five minutes before bed.' The Against All Odds Girl neither believes me or cares. 'That was so fun,' she says (when she has decided, not I, that she has had enough). 'Can I have a hot chocolate when I get home?' 'Sure,' I say, making a mental note to use the hot chocolate bribe to get the boys home tomorrow, when they have their snow day which isn't today.

A message pings up from the boys' school (not from the lady about the plastic horse) to say the afternoon off school, in which they won't get blacklisted for not attending lessons but the Against All Odds Girl will, is scheduled from 2.30pm. This means that I must be 'fun mum' for them (it may involve more high octane snowboarding stunts) but not her. I am on a rotation where I must pull out the giggles and the good times when it suits the schools but not me, because my time is not up for question.

It's the allotted time, on the second snow day, which belongs to the boys but not the girl, and the boys come off the screens that their school says are both bad for them and good for them. I don't tell the Against All Odds Girl that the boys are off to ride the white stuff because she will get cross and not just about the departure of the horse that isn't real.

We sneak off with the sledges and the puppy, who is on her third sledging trip and can't work out why there are different members of the family attending each day. I am halfway down the hill on the plastic tray and pretending I am in Méribel about to go off to La Folie Douce when the phone rings. 'Why did you go without me?' I can hear the Husband snorting in the background because he obviously has been told to place the call. 'Because you have lessons and you had your snow day, yesterday.'

'But you could have waited one more hour for me to come.' 'Right,' I say, because the image of downing a beer and dancing on a table at a ski resort is fast disappearing and the reality that I am on a hill in north Essex is kicking in. 'I'm coming now,' she says. I am freezing and my fingers are turning blue. The boys say they are off. 'Thanks guys,' I shout, as they head home to warm up. I am left in the field, not Méribel, with three sledges and a puppy that has decided it is more fun to run slightly ahead of the sledge and try and break her leg in the process.

The flicky hair girl arrives. The green in her eyes is getting darker, which means she is angry, like really angry. She grabs the sledge and stomps up the hill. It doesn't help that she has realised that the Middle Child has taken her gloves and they are soaking wet. She does a kamikaze downhill sledge to annoy me and I try to smile so that we can just get through it. We do this a few more times, until again she decides she wants to go home. 'Can I have a hot chocolate?' 'Yes, and anything else you want, too,' I say out loud because I will do anything at this point to be at home and off the snowy hill.

We get back to the homestead where there are wet ski trousers, gloves and hats on the floor (ready for me, not them, to pick up) and the children say to me, 'Is it a snow day tomorrow?' 'No,' I say (not knowing whether it is or not) because if I have to do anymore sledging I will properly lose my 's**t' and tell the schools where they can put their 'fun snow day rotation'.

Sno-way we are staying indoors – Tabitha Peters, aged 12

19 February, 2021 – February Half-Term = 'Date walks' and Bubble Gum

Prime Minister, Boris Johnson, chairs a virtual G7 summit in which member countries agree to provide an extra £5bn funding to help accelerate the distribution of COVID-19 vaccines to the world's poorest countries.

The High Court rules that Health Secretary, Matt Hancock, 'breached his legal obligations' by failing to reveal details of contracts signed by the Department of Health and Social Care during the pandemic.

Figures from the Office for National Statistics show that COVID rates continued to fall in the week ending 12 February.

The R number is estimated to be between 0.6 and 0.9, a slight fall on the previous week's figures.

(Wikipedia, 2021)

There are only two options for February half-term: A. Go on a series of 'date walks'; B. Start ripping out rooms in the homestead for entertainment. I can't think of a third option, so we are doing both, simultaneously.

The first day of the hols, the Middle Child calls in the mates for his 'date walk' which means I leave the Teenager and the Against All Odds Girl at home, for fear of being illegal. They eat crisps and some out-of-date chocolate because the Husband is ripping out the upstairs bathroom, which involves some hacksawing and dust, lots of dust. He doesn't think to close the adjoining bedroom doors because we like to make extra work for ourselves and the two children that aren't on the 'date walk' don't care either because they are head down in some Walkers prawn cocktail crisps. I am wondering when the demolished rooms move on to stage two because the first ripped out room has been in a sort of lockdown of its own since last summer. The Husband has remembered to close the door on that one because he knows 'out of sight, out of mind' is better for our combined mental health. This doesn't apply when it comes to dust because you can't see it - but I can feel it.

The Middle Child returns jubilant after the outdoors, social distanced walk with the 'fwend', which basically involves a mud slide down a bank and a Bear Grylls rope swing adventure, in which the tree it is suspended from creaks louder and louder at each rotation - but it's worth it for the 'off screen' time which the school encourages, in between the times when they tell them they have to be on the screen.

The plumber appears and the Against All Odds Girl is as exultant as I feel at the prospect of progress. 'Would you like a coffee or a tea?' she asks. 'No, that's kind I won't but thanks,' says the plumber, who has long hair like Rapunzel, which in his WhatsApp photo he pulls over his face, like a unique face mask. When you discuss mixer taps you do so with a man that has no eyes, just hair. A few moments later I ask the same question because my mother has trained me well and I have to offer someone a cuppa if they are in my house. He looks at me, incredulous, 'No thanks, I've got my thermos, I am not accepting tea or coffee during COVID.' And, with that, the very British pastime of breaking the ice with Yorkshire Tea is removed forever from our national psyche.

The puppy looks up and wonders who she will be going on a walking date with today. It's the Teenager's turn, although the Teenager's friend has a brother in the same year as the Middle Child, so we agree they can all go but walk distanced. The Against All Odds Girl is angry that there is no sister to strut with, so I agree she can eat the remainder of the prawn cocktail crisps at home and lick the dust off the floorboards, again unsupervised, because the Husband is putting on some plaster board to the room that is permanently locked down. Again, this is progress, but he is distracted by work calls, even though he is on holiday, because you can't really be on holiday during the pandemic when you work at home all the time and there is no holiday that you can actually go on.

I return home from the Teenager/Middle Child walk in which both pairs refuse to speak to me and walk in a social distanced, Pied Piper style away from each other – not because they are ever so compliant but because it is now uncool to walk with your brother and his friend. It's a tapered effect according to age brackets, although the exception is the dog and myself, being the ancient one and the youngest one, that haven't been picked for the team.

The Against All Odds Girl is having a proper meltdown because she hasn't been on any 'date walks' and/or left the house and she can't hear her favourite programme because there are various drilling and hammering sounds going on. She is also annoyed because she caught me eating her last strawberry bubble gum and I have had to order a bubble gum dispenser machine to make up for it, because I can't be bothered to go to the village shop and that's the closest replacement I can get to it on Amazon. We get home to unwrap the parcel, which has been delivered by a man who is also concerned about COVID because he hurls it over the hedge so as not to touch us, having driven miles and not worried about his carbon footprint in the process – but you can't have one or the other during these times and the environment has to give when you need candy.

She opens it up and we are teleported into an arcade where you are forced to part with silver coins to get some of the E-stuff inside. She seems happy but I know her, and I can see her start to chew and says, 'I still haven't seen a friend,' while at the same time moulding the gum over the end of her tongue. 'Well, you know what, neither have I and, what do you expect me to do, go on three walks a day with different people?' 'Yes,' she says. I consider the options again: A. Be a good parent and tell her where to go; B. Take the sensible option and call in a girl for a walking date, so I don't have to deal with the whining. I fall into the category of 'B' and dial up a good friend, who is also a 'B' option kinda girl and we fix a time. 'Bring the chewing gum,' she says, and I do because I realise I am not the Pied Piper or an A-grade parent, I am just weary, weary of lockdown and weary of dust and demolition.

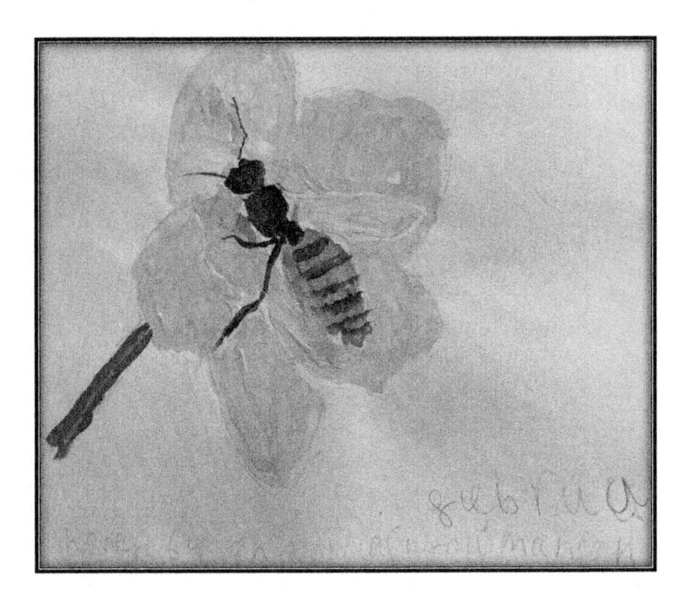

Honey Bee – Oli Manson, aged 6

25 February, 2021 – Boris Bingo and Birthday Science Lessons

The UK's COVID alert level is lowered from five to four as the threat of the virus overwhelming the NHS has receded.

Her Majesty The Queen takes part in a video call with health leaders helping to deliver the vaccine, during which she urges people to get the vaccine when it is offered to them.

(Wikipedia, 2021)

I'm playing 'Boris Bingo' with my work pals when the PM announces that schools are re-opening on 8 March. You imagine these defining moments of life to be 'filtered' of reality. We want to visualise ourselves in *The Truman Show* (pretending it's the bit when it all seems perfect but Jim Carrey hasn't as yet clocked this can't be for real) and there is a smiling, hat-wearing girl cycling past, as the sun rises. The reality is different. I am praying the floppy-haired one says, 'Next slide, please,' so I can win a Lindt chocolate bunny, while looking down at my Smart phone in an attempt to work out how to edit the bingo card online, when he utters the hallowed words that parents across the land have been waiting to hear for months: 'Schools are re-opening.'

I look up from the Bingo sheet, having missed the moment (and if you are asking, I didn't win) and feel like I want to re-wind or hit pause and just bask in the gloriousness of it. I have a flashback to the time when the child (well, I have three, but when you have more than your allotted few you just have to mesh the memories into one, so it's the 1x3 rule of thumb) takes his or her first steps (don't judge me for not remembering which one it was). I hope that I am the mother that is sitting in a meadow full of daisies and the child is clothed in striped dungarees and takes their first pitter patter, beaming at you while you hold out your hand (having temporarily put down your pork pie) and you embrace and hug in the joyousness of it all.

What actually happens is the 1x3 reaches out for the bathroom spray bottle, as I try to remove some limescale from the tub and I am swearing under my breath at the mundanity of it all – I only realise the first steps have been taken because I can't work out how he/she has teleported themselves to my side. This is what happens with the BoJo words – I want it to be perfect but it isn't and I have to console myself that back in the room of adult land we should be pleased and happy and not kicking ourselves that we were not focused and sitting in a hoovered armchair free of crisps at the time or looking down at some words including, 'Tier 5' 'Draconian' and 'Flatten the curve' when it happens (I mean, I was never going to win with that line-up).

And so, it is, that just like that the homeschooling has an end date. The calendar has a mark on it which says, 'Go back to school, suckers.' The Husband and I are jubilant, we want to hug and cry at the same time. The children look at us and wonder why we are so joyful. 'You're going back to school.' 'Are you serious?' the 1x3 say. 'Yep,' we confirm, and they nod in an 'OK' my time's up and I've had a good innings kinda way and slink back to their screens, on which they have liveth on for most of lockdown.

The reality of the life that we are in, not *The Truman Show* one, is brought back again, with a thud, when the next day the Middle Child is in science, in which he learns about the correct names of the human sex organs. 'Oh god, it's the penis lesson,' says the Middle Child, downgrading the scientific vocabulary to just that. I try not to snigger because I am his 45-year old mother, but you know it's a universal truth that you will laugh about 'toilet humour' until the day you die. The teacher, who is trying to keep her s**t together and not guffaw, is showing them a clip of human fertilisation. I mean not that actual bit (come on) but the science part when the tadpole things (yes, I know the correct term) swim to the egg. The teacher asks them to write notes. The group chat that the pre-pubescent (well most of them) 11-year olds are looking at and not the video sensation goes like this:

'Yeah I ain't watching that' (Girl 1 – who sends muchos smiling faces with horns emojis)

'I JUST WATCHED THE FIRST 3 SECONDS I CAN'T' (Girl 2 - whose finger is stuck on Caps lock)

'EWWW' (Girl 2 – again … trying to get her disgust across)

'AHHH' (Different girl, same emojis)

'Well we gonna have to' (Girl 1 - again)

'I'm not writing notes' (Anonymous)

It's the Middle Child's birthday, when he is learning about how he was conceived, which seems apt. He looks up at me as I try to place some chocolate fingers around the side of his birthday cake to hide the defects of a wonkily cut Victoria sponge (which is light and fluffy, I can tell you). 'This is gross,' he says, because the boys seem so outraged about the birds and the bees, they can't contribute to the WhatsApp chat of the pre-teens, whereas the girls are all over it (see above). Much like life really.

I think his life lessons of late have been rather coloured by the fact he is at home. I mean, if he was in the classroom, where he should be, he wouldn't be scrolling through purple horn emojis while he watches the sperm swim.

When it's religious studies and the teacher is talking about the life of Jesus, I am hoovering and the Middle Child is 'shushing me' in case he misses the significance of the birth, death, resurrection bit (although perhaps he needn't worry because he is getting all the knowledge he needs on that one from the science teacher, bar the rising again part).

The cake is done, glued together with chocolate fingers and a green ribbon I found down the back of the sofa, along with the stale crisps, which I sat on while doing the Boris Bingo. I feel it must be 4pm because I have already done enough, on this the day of his birth anniversary, because I have been up since 6am watching the Middle Child unwrap a metal detector and don't forget I have also attended senior school science and religious education, too.

Getting ready for school (again) – the Against All Odds Girl, aged 8

MARCH, 2021

4 March, 2021 – World Book Day, Ben Fogle and Maths Tests

The Medicines and Healthcare Products Regulatory Agency issues guidelines allowing fast-tracked approval for new versions of existing COVID-19 vaccines developed to fight variants, similar to the existing rules for annual flu vaccines.

Public Health England has added a new COVID variant to its watchlist after 16 cases were identified of a strain with similarities to the South African and Brazilian variants.

Security services confirm that three terror plots against UK targets have been foiled since the start of the pandemic.

David Ashford, the Isle of Man's Health Minister, announces that all adults on the island will receive their first COVID vaccination by the end of May. An increase in vaccine deliveries means it will shortly be possible to administer up to 1,000 vaccinations per day.

The Big Festival, cancelled in 2020 due to COVID-19, is confirmed for 27–29 August 2021.

(Wikipedia, 2021)

The Against All Odds Girl is excited, well let's be real, ecstatic is closer to her state of mind, about World Book Day. There are some benefits to lockdown and homeschooling and I had hoped that skipping the dressing-up day would be one of them, but, no, like many of the blows of the past 12 months. She wants to go to the 'skool, skool' (dressed as a farm girl) with the keyworker gang, which is a bit like *The Breakfast Club*, bar the teen bit: detainment in a classroom with a mish mash of kids you didn't know before, but now you do, including the finer details of why they have a mole on their face to their thoughts on 'butter or no butter' in their sandwiches.

She is Fern from *Charlotte's Web* which involves taking last year's *Annie* costume of a red dress and white collar and tucking it into some hand-me down dungarees while stripping a shower gel and body lotion set of a gingham ribbon and transplanting it onto her pony tail. We arrive at 'The Breakfast Club' to see the PE teacher walking the other way. I am assuming he is *The Boy in the Dress* because he has a blonde wig on and a short skirt, either that or he has wrongly assumed it's Saturday night and his wife is out.

The Against All Odds Girl has made a web out of cocktail sticks, packing tape and some discoloured string. She greets the music teacher, who dispenses hand gel as well as playing in a symphony orchestra and pulls out the DIY web. He misfires while congratulating her on her creation and the sticky stuff seeps into the cocktail sticks. She is unsure whether to laugh or cry but I shove her forward because I don't want to deal with the fallout of a costume gone wrong and, anyway, I am trying to get another glimpse of the PE teacher who was last seen walking towards the playing field in a pair of stilettos.

While I deal with my parental decisions, I look at a social media post by Ben Fogle, who is sitting by an outdoor fire looking cold. He's plugging his *New Lives In The Wild* series. I love it because it helps me to feel normal (who wouldn't when they watch the Yorkshire Shepherdess remember all the names of her nine free-ranging children). I am aglow with my own comparisons, knowing the first and middle names of the Against All Odds Girl and today of her book character, too. I am therefore a good parent.

Meanwhile, Ben, who has cold toes, is asking us, 'Not to judge a book by its cover,' but this is difficult when you are making up wild stories in your head about the PE teacher and his desire to dress as a cheerleader.

The Middle Child is learning about the 'one child' policy in China. He is asked to read from a passage in which he finds out about the pressures on only children. 'I got 76% in a maths test and my parents took my pocket money away from me for a week,' (this is the Chinese child, not the Middle Child - I mean, come on, if he got 76% we would be having a party, not withdrawing polymer notes). It goes on to say how they must study before, at and after school (the Chinese children, not the ones sat in my homestead).

The Middle Child looks shocked, it's the same face he gives me when he is in the 'penis' lesson, which is kind of interlinked because his next question to me is, 'How do they ensure they only have one child?' I try to re-frame the learning points, so that he appreciates that he would work harder if he was born in China in the late 1970s and that it is good to study because otherwise you might be cashless, but he wants to concentrate on the ability to produce the 1 and not the 1x3 that we have. I don't think I can face this conversation, particularly as while he is in his geography lesson and learning about Chinese population, I am making a sausage casserole.

The Teenager is oblivious of World Book Day because he is in a maths test with a teacher that is dressed as themselves.

Question 9:
The radius of a circular flower bed is 30.5cm.
Work out the circumference of the flower bed.
Give your answer in terms of Pi in its simplest form.

I'm wondering if the Yorkshire Shepherdess deals with this 1x9 or if she just tells them to go and breathe fresh air so she can make a stew instead. I think the latter. The Teenager is looking at me for help and I stare back with a look that says, 'Well you should have revised your 3.14 calculation instead of watching Ben Fogle [again, but this time in *Inside Chernobyl* … he gets around] until 10.30pm.' He looks back while yawning and moving on to the next question, which is about using the equation to work out the volume of a jar but he doesn't know much about that either, although he can tell us about one of the worst nuclear disasters of our time and he can also provide details on when Fogle is going to be on TV tomorrow and the day after that. I think this is potentially more useful, so I bring him a hot chocolate as an affirmation to not caring about Pi or garden measurements.

I'm slightly distracted, while trying to remember the names of my children, by a WhatsApp from my pals who share some commentary from the Family Lockdown Tips & Ideas Facebook group (which I left some months ago on account of the number of rainbows their children drew).

A mum writes:

I know for most families, there is great relief and thankfulness for the return of school and that routine …
But …
Are there any of you who have now had a chance to try home education and it has actually helped you decide that you WANT to do it full-time?
Just wondering:

There are 1.2k comments but the one that stands out is:

*I'd rather cover myself in honey and staple my t*ts to a beehive*

And to that I say, fair play my friend, fair play.

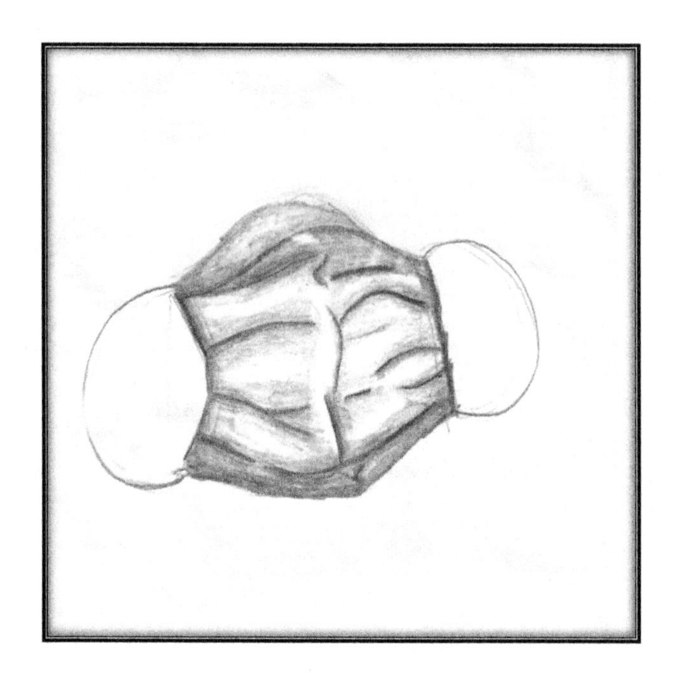

Compulsory mask wearing – Sophie Williams, aged 12

8 March, 2021 – Miracles Can Happen

The children did go to:

S
C
H
O
O
L

AFTERWORD

I continue to document my family life in my blog, *The Paroking Diaries*, published on Facebook. I hope I have given families like my own comfort and hope that this unique and unprecedented period of our children's lives and education hasn't gone unnoticed or unrecorded. I would like to thank you all for your lovely messages and I take particular pleasure from those that have approached me to thank me for being honest about how family life and homeschooling actually rolled during the time the children didn't go to school. This book is for all of you. x

It's a wrap - Tabitha Peters, aged 12

Printed in Great Britain
by Amazon

70298346R00132